The Lady of Lyons

Edward Bulwer Lytton

Contents

THE LADY OF LYONS

BY

Edward Bulwer Lytton

To the author of "Ion."

Whose genius and example have alike contributed towards the regeneration of The National Drama,

This play is inscribed.

PREFACE.

An indistinct recollection of the very pretty little tale, called "The Bellows-Mender," suggested the plot of this Drama. The incidents are, however, greatly altered from those in the tale, and the characters entirely re-cast.

Having long had a wish to illustrate certain periods of the French history, so, in the selection of the date in which the scenes of this play are laid, I saw that the era of the Republic was that in which the incidents were rendered most probable, in which the probationary career of the hero could well be made sufficiently rapid for dramatic effect, and in which the character of the time itself was depicted by the agencies necessary to the conduct of the narrative. For during the early years of the first and most brilliant successes of the French Republic, in the general ferment of society, and the brief equalization of ranks, Claude's high-placed love; his ardent feelings, his unsettled principles (the struggle between which makes the passion of this drama), his ambition, and his career, were phenomena that characterized the age, and in which the spirit of the nation went along with the extravagance of the individual.

The play itself was composed with a twofold object. In the first place, sympathizing with the enterprise of Mr. Macready, as Manager of Covent Garden, and believing that many of the higher interests of the Drama were involved in the success or failure of an enterprise equally hazardous and disinterested, I felt, if I may so presume to express myself, something of the Brotherhood of Art; and it was only for Mr. Macready to think it possible that I might serve him in order to induce me to make the attempt.

Secondly, in that attempt I was mainly anxious to see whether or not, after the comparative failure on the stage of "The Duchess de la Valliere," certain critics had truly declared that it was not in my power to attain the art of dramatic construction and theatrical effect. I felt, indeed, that it was in this that a writer, accustomed to the narrative class of composition, would have the most both to learn and unlearn. Accordingly, it was to the development of the plot and the arrangement of the incidents that I directed my chief attention;--and I sought to throw whatever belongs to poetry less into the diction and the "felicity of words" than into the construction of the story, the creation of the characters, and the spirit of the pervading sentiment.

The authorship of the play was neither avowed nor suspected until the play had established itself in public favor. The announcement of my name was the signal for attacks, chiefly political, to which it is now needless to refer. When a work has outlived for some time the earlier hostilities of criticism, there comes a new race of critics to which a writer may, for the most part, calmly trust for a fair consideration, whether of the faults or the merits of his performance.

DRAMATIS PERSONAE.

BEAUSEANT, a rich gentleman of Lyons, in love with, and refused by, Pauline Deschappelles   MR. ELTON.

GLAVIS, his friend, also a rejected suitor to Pauline   MR. MEADOWS.

COLONEL (afterwards General) DAMAS, cousin to Mme. Deschappelles, and an officer in the French army   MR. BARTLEY.

MONSIEUR DESCHAPPELLES, a Lyonnese merchant father to Pauline   MR. STRICKLAND.

GASPAR   MR. DIDDEAR.

CLAUDE MELNOTTE   MR. MACREADY.

FIRST OFFICER   MR. HOWE.

SECOND OFFICER   MR. PRITCHARD.

THIRD OFFICER   MR. ROBERTS.

Servants, Notary, etc.

MADAME DESCHAPPELLES	MRS. W. CLIFFORD.
PAULINE, her daughter	MISS HELEN FAUCIT.
THE WIDOW MELNOTTE, mother to Claude	MRS. GRIFFITH.
JANET, the innkeeper's daughter	MRS. EAST.
MARIAN, maid to Pauline	MISS GARRICK.

Scene--Lyons and the neighborhood.

Time--1795-1798

First performed on Thursday, the 15th of February, 1838, at Covent Garden Theatre.

THE LADY OF LYONS;
or,
LOVE AND PRIDE.

ACT I.--SCENE I.

A room in the house of M. DESCHAPPELLES, at Lyons. PAULINE reclining
on a sofa; MARIAN, her maid, fanning her--Flowers and notes on a table
beside the sofa--MADAME DESCHAPPELLES seated--The gardens are seen from
the open window.

Mme. Deschap. Marian, put that rose a little more to the left.--[MARIAN
alters the position of a rose in PAULINE's hair.]--Ah, so!--that
improves the hair,--the tournure, the j'e ne sais quoi!--You are
certainly very handsome, child!--quite my style;--I don't wonder that
you make such a sensation!--Old, young, rich, and poor, do homage to the
Beauty of Lyons!--Ah, we live again in our children,--especially when
they have our eyes and complexion!

Pauline [languidly]. Dear mother, you spoil your Pauline!--[Aside.] I
wish I knew who sent me these flowers!

Mme. Deschap. No, child!--If I praise you, it is only to inspire you with a proper ambition.--You are born to make a great marriage.--Beauty is valuable or worthless according as you invest the property to the best advantage. Marian, go and order the carriage! [Exit MARIAN.

Pauline. Who can it be that sends me, every day, these beautiful flowers?--how sweet they are!

Enter Servant.

Servant. Monsieur Beauseant, Madam.

Mme. Deschap. Let him enter. Pauline, this is another offer!--I know it is!--Your father should engage an additional clerk to keep the account-book of your conquests.

Enter BEAUSEANT.

Beau. Ah, ladies how fortunate I am to find you at home!--[Aside.] How lovely she looks!--It is a great sacrifice I make in marrying into a family in trade!--they will be eternally grateful!--[Aloud.] Madam, you will permit me a word with your charming daughter.--[Approaches PAULINE, who rises disdainfully.]--Mademoiselle, I have ventured to wait upon you, in a hope that you must long since have divined. Last night, when you outshone all the beauty of Lyons, you completed your conquest over me! You know that my fortune is not exceeded by any estate in the province,--you know that, but for the Revolution, which has defrauded me of my titles, I should be noble. May I, then, trust that you will not reject my alliance? I offer you my hand and heart.

Pauline aside.] He has the air of a man who confers a favor!--[Aloud.] Sir, you are very condescending--I thank you humbly; but, being duly sensible of my own demerits, you must allow me to decline the honor you propose. [Curtsies, and turns away.

Beau. Decline! Impossible!--you are not serious!--Madam, suffer me to appeal to you. I am a suitor for your daughter's hand--the settlements shall be worthy of her beauty and my station. May I wait on M. Deschappelles?

Mme. Deschap. M. Deschappelles never interferes in the domestic arrangements,--you are very obliging. If you were still a marquis, or if my daughter were intended to marry a commoner,--why, perhaps, we might give you the preference.

Beau. A commoner!--we are all commoners in France now.

Mme. Deschap. In France, yes; but there is a nobility still left in the other countries in Europe. We are quite aware of your good qualities, and don't doubt that you will find some lady more suitable to your pretensions. We shall be always happy to see you as an acquaintance, M. Beauseant!--My dear child, the carriage will be here presently.

Beau. Say no more, madam!--say no more!--[Aside.] Refused! and by a merchant's daughter!--refused! It will be all over Lyons before sunset!--I will go and bury myself in my chateau, study philosophy, and turn woman-hater. Refused! they ought to be sent to a madhouse!-- Ladies, I have the honor to wish you a very good morning. [Exit.

Mme. Deschap. How forward these men are!--I think, child, we kept up our dignity. Any girl, however inexperienced, knows how to accept an offer, but it requires a vast deal of address to refuse one with proper condescension and disdain. I used to practise it at school with the dancing-master.

Enter DAMAS.

Damas. Good morning, cousin Deschappelles.--Well, Pauline, are you recovered from last night's ball?--So many triumphs must be very fatiguing. Even M. Glavis sighed most piteously when you departed; but that might be the effect of the supper.

Pauline. M. Glavis, indeed!

Mme. Deschap. M. Glavis?--as if my daughter would think of M. Glavis!

Damas. Hey-day!--why not?--His father left him a very pretty fortune, and his birth is higher than yours, cousin Deschappelles. But perhaps you are looking to M. Beauseant,--his father was a marquis before the Revolution.

Pauline. M. Beauseant!--Cousin, you delight in tormenting me!

Mme. Deschap. Don't mind him, Pauline!--Cousin Damas, you have no susceptibility of feeling,--there is a certain indelicacy in all your ideas.--M. Beauseant knows already that he is no match for my daughter!

Damas. Pooh! pooh! one would think you intended your daughter to marry a prince!

Mme. Deschap. Well, and if I did?--what then?--Many a foreign prince--

Damas [interrupting her]. Foreign prince!--foreign fiddlestick!--you ought to be ashamed of such nonsense at your time of life.

Mme. Deschap. My time of life!--That is an expression never applied to any lady till she is sixty-nine and three-quarters;--and only then by the clergyman of the parish.

Enter Servant.

Servant. Madame, the carriage is at the door. [Exit.

Mme. Deschap. Come, child, put on your bonnet--you really have a very thorough-bred air--not at all like your poor father.--[Fondly]. Ah, you little coquette! when a young lady is always making mischief, it is a sure sign that she takes after her mother!

Pauline. Good day, cousin Damas--and a better humor to you.--[Going back to the table and taking the flowers]. Who could have sent me these flowers? [Exeunt PAULINE and MADAME DESCHAPPELLES.

Damas. That would be an excellent girl if her head had not been turned. I fear she is now become incorrigible! Zounds, what a lucky fellow I am to be still a bachelor! They may talk of the devotion of the sex--but the most faithful attachment in life is that of a woman in love--with herself. [Exit.

SCENE II.

The exterior of a small Village Inn--sign, the Golden Lion--A few leagues from Lyons, which is seen at a distance.

Beau. [behind the scenes.] Yes, you may bait the horses; we shall rest here an hour.

Enter BEAUSEANT and GLAVIS.

Gla. Really, my dear Beauseant, consider that I have promised to spend a day or two with you at your chateau, that I am quite at your mercy for my entertainment,--and yet you are as silent and as gloomy as a mute at a funeral, or an Englishman at a party of pleasure.

Beau. Bear with me!--the fact is that I am miserable.

Gla. You--the richest and gayest bachelor in Lyons?

Beau. It is because I am a bachelor that I am miserable.--Thou knowest
Pauline--the only daughter of the rich merchant, Mons. Deschappelles?

Gla. Know her?--who does not?--as pretty as Venus, and as proud as Juno.

Beau. Her taste is worse than her pride.--[Drawing himself up.] Know,
Glavis, she has actually refused me!

Gla. [aside]. So she has me!--very consoling! In all cases of
heart-ache, the application of another man's disappointment draws
out the pain and allays the irritation.--[Aloud.] Refused you! and
wherefore?

Beau. I know not, unless it be because the Revolution swept away my
father's title of Marquis,--and she will not marry a commoner. Now, as
we have no noblemen left in France,--as we are all citizens and equals,
she can only hope that, in spite of the war, some English Milord or
German Count will risk his life, by coming to Lyons, that this fille du
Roturier may condescend to accept him. Refused me, and with scorn!--By
Heaven, I'll not submit to it tamely:--I'm in a perfect fever of
mortification and rage.--Refuse me, indeed!

Gla. Be comforted, my dear fellow,--I will tell you a secret. For the
same reason she refused ME!

Beau. You!--that's a very different matter! But give me your hand,
Glavis,--we'll think of some plan to humble her. Mille diables! I should

like to see her married to a strolling player!

Enter Landlord and his Daughter from the Inn.

Land. Your servant, citizen Beauseant,--servant, Sir. Perhaps you will take dinner before you proceed to your chateau; our larder is most plentifully supplied.

Beau. I have no appetite.

Gla. Nor I. Still it is bad travelling on an empty stomach. What have you got? [Takes and looks over the bill of fare.]

[Shout without.] "Long live the Prince!--Long live the Prince!"

Beau. The Prince!--what Prince is that? I thought we had no princes left in France.

Land. Ha, ha! the lads always call him Prince. He has just won the prize in the shooting-match, and they are taking him home in triumph.

Beau. Him! and who's Mr. Him?

Land. Who should he be but the pride of the village, Claude Melnotte?--Of course you have heard of Claude Melnotte?

Gla. [giving back the bill of fare.] Never had that honor. Soup--ragout of hare--roast chicken, and, in short, all you have!

Beau. The son of old Alelnotte, the gardener?

Land. Exactly so--a wonderful young man.

Beau. How, wonderful?--Are his cabbages better than other people's

Land. Nay, he don't garden any more; his father left him well off. He's only a genus.

Gla. A what?

Land. A genus!--a man who can do everything in life except anything that's useful--that's a genus.

Beau. You raise my curiosity;--proceed.

Land. Well, then, about four years ago, old Melnotte died, and left his son well to do in the world. We then all observed that a great change came over young Claude: he took to reading and Latin, and hired a professor from Lyons, who had so much in his head that he was forced to wear a great full-bottom wig to cover it. Then he took a fencing-master, and a dancing-master, and a music-master; and then he learned to paint; and at last it was said that young Claude was to go to Paris, and set up for a painter. The lads laughed at him at first; but he is a stout fellow, is Claude, and as brave as a lion, and soon taught them to laugh the wrong side of their mouths; and now all the boys swear by him, and all the girls pray for him.

Beau. A promising youth, certainly! And why do they call him Prince?

Land. Partly because he is at the head of them all, and partly because he has such a proud way with him, and wears such fine clothes--and, in short, looks like a prince.

Beau. And what could have turned the foolish fellow's brain? The Revolution, I suppose?

Land. Yes--the revolution that turns us all topsy-turvy--the revolution of Love.

Beau. Romantic young Corydon! And with whom is he in love?

Land. Why--but it is a secret, gentlemen.

Beau. Oh! certainly.

Land. Why, then, I hear from his mother, good soul! that it is no less a person than the Beauty of Lyons, Pauline Deschappelles.

Beau. and Glavis. Ha, ha!--Capital!

Land. You may laugh, but it is as true as I stand here.

Beau. And what does the Beauty of Lyons say to his suit?

Land. Lord, sir, she never even condescended to look at him, though when he was a boy he worked in her father's garden.

Beau. Are you sure of that?

Land. His mother says that Mademoiselle does not know him by sight.

Beau. [taking Glavis aside]. I have hit it,--I have it; here is our revenge! Here is a prince for our haughty damsel. Do you take me?

Gla. Deuce take me if I do!

Beau. Blockhead!--it's as clear as a map. What if we could make this elegant clown pass himself off as a foreign prince?--lend him money, clothes, equipage for the purpose?--make him propose to Pauline?--marry

Pauline? Would it not be delicious?

Gla. Ha, ha!--Excellent! But how shall we support the necessary expenses of his highness?

Beau. Pshaw! Revenge is worth a much larger sacrifice than a few hundred louis;--as for details, my valet is the trustiest fellow, in the world, and shall have the appointment of his highness's establishment. Let's go to him at once, and see if he be really this Admirable Crichton.

Gla. With all my heart;--but the dinner?

Beau. Always thinking of dinner! Hark ye, landlord; how far is it to young Melnotte's cottage? I should like to see such a prodigy.

Land. Turn down the lane,--then strike across the common,--and you will see his mother's cottage.

Beau. True, he lives with his mother.--[Aside.] We will not trust to an old woman's discretion; better send for him hither. I'll just step in and write a note. Come, Glavis.

Gla. Yes,--Beauseant, Glavis, and Co., manufacturers of princes, wholesale and retail,--an uncommonly genteel line of business. But why so grave?

Beau. You think only of the sport,--I of the revenge. [Exeunt within the Inn.

SCENE III.

The interior of MELNOTTE'S cottage; flowers placed here and there; a
guitar on an oaken table, with a portfolio, etc.; a picture on an easel,
covered by a curtain; fencing foils crossed over the mantelpiece; an
attempt at refinement in site of the homeliness of the furniture, etc.;
a staircase to the right conducts to the upper story.

[Shout without]. "Long live Claude Melnotte!" "Long live the Prince!"

The Widow Mel. Hark!--there's my dear son;--carried off the prize, I'm
sure; and now he'll want to treat them all.

Claude Mel. [opening the door]. What! you will not come in, my friends!
Well, well, there's a trifle to make merry elsewhere. Good day to you
all,--good day!

[Shout]. "Hurrah! Long live Prince Claude!"

Enter CLAUDE MELNOTTE, with a rifle in his hand.

Mel. Give me joy, dear mother!--I've won the prize!--never missed one
shot! Is it not handsome, this gun?

Widow. Humph!--Well, what is it worth, Claude?

Mel. Worth! What is a riband worth to a soldier? Worth! everything!
Glory is priceless!

Widow. Leave glory to great folks. Ah! Claude, Claude, castles in the
air cost a vast deal to keep up! How is all this to end? What good does
it do thee to learn Latin, and sing songs, and play on the guitar, and

fence, and dance, and paint pictures? All very fine; but what does it bring in?

Mel. Wealth! wealth, my mother! Wealth to the mind--wealth to the heart--high thoughts--bright dreams--the hope of fame--the ambition to be worthier to love Pauline.

Widow. My poor son!--The young lady will never think of thee.

Mel. Do the stars think of us? Yet if the prisoner see them shine into his dungeon, wouldst thou bid him turn away from their lustre? Even so from this low cell, poverty, I lift my eyes to Pauline and forget my chains.--[Goes to the picture and draws aside the curtain.]

See, this is her image--painted from memory. Oh, how the canvas wrongs her!--[Takes up the brush and throws it aside.] I shall never be a painter! I can paint no likeness but one, and that is above all art. I would turn soldier--France needs soldiers! But to leave the air that Pauline breathes! What is the hour?--so late? I will tell thee a secret, mother. Thou knowest that for the last six weeks I have sent every day the rarest flowers to Pauline?--she wears them. I have seen them on her breast. Ah, and then the whole universe seemed filled with odors! I have now grown more bold--I have poured my worship into poetry--I have sent the verses to Pauline--I have signed them with my own name. My messenger ought to--be back by this time. I bade him wait for the answer.

Widow. And what answer do you expect, Claude?

Mel. That which the Queen of Navarre sent to the poor troubadour:--"Let me see the Oracle that can tell nations I am beautiful!" She will admit me. I shall hear her speak--I shall meet her eyes--I shall read upon her cheek the sweet thoughts that translate themselves into blushes.

Then--then, oh, then--she may forget that I am the peasant's son!.

Widow. Nay, if she will but hear thee talk, Claude?

Mel. I foresee it all. She will tell me that desert is the true rank. She will give me a badge--a flower--a glove! Oh rapture! I shall join the armies of the republic--I shall rise--I shall win a name that beauty will not blush to hear. I shall return with the right to say to her--"See, how love does not level the proud, but raise the--humble!" Oh, how my heart swells within me!--Oh, what glorious prophets of the future are youth and hope!

[Knock at the door.]

Widow. Come in.

Enter GASPAR.

Mel. Welcome, Gaspar, welcome. Where is the letter? Why do you turn away, man? where is the letter? [GASPAR gives him one.] This! This is mine, the one I intrusted to thee. Didst thou not leave it?

Gaspar. Yes, I left it.

Mel. My own verses returned to me. Nothing else!

Gaspar. Thou wilt be proud to hear how thy messenger was honored. For thy sake, Melnotte, I have borne that which no Frenchman can bear without disgrace.

Mel. Disgrace, Gaspar! Disgrace?

Gaspar. I gave thy letter to the porter, who passed it from lackey to lackey till it reached the lady it was meant for.

Mel. It reached her, then; you are sure of that! It reached her,--well, well!

Gaspar. It reached her, and was returned to me with blows. Dost hear, Melnotte? with blows! Death! are we slaves still, that we are to be thus dealt with, we peasants?

Mel. With blows? No, Gaspar, no; not blows!

Gaspar. I could show thee the marks if it were not so deep a shame to bear them. The lackey who tossed thy letter into the mire swore that his lady and her mother never were so insulted. What could thy letter contain, Claude?

Mel. [looking over the letter]. Not a line that a serf might not have written to an empress. No, not one.

Gaspar. They promise thee the same greeting they gave me, if thou wilt pass that way. Shall we endure this, Claude?

Mel. [wringing GASPAR's hand]. Forgive me, the fault was mine, I have brought this on thee; I will not forget it; thou shalt be avenged! The heartless insolence!

Gaspar. Thou art moved, Melnotte; think not of me; I would go through fire and water to serve thee; but,--a blow! It is not the bruise that galls,--it is the blush, Melnotte.

Mel. Say, what message?--How insulted!--Wherefore?--What the offence?

Gaspar. Did you not write to Pauline Deschappelles, the daughter of the rich merchant?

Mel. Well?

Gaspar. And are you not a peasant--a gardener's son?--that was the offence. Sleep on it, Melnotte. Blows to a French citizen, blows! [Exit.

Widow. Now you are cured, Claude!

Mel. tearing the letter. So do I scatter her image to the winds--I will stop her in the open streets--I will insult her--I will beat her menial ruffians--I will--[Turns suddenly to Widow.] Mother, am I humpbacked--deformed--hideous? Widow. You!

Mel. A coward--a thief--a liar?

Widow. You!

Mel. Or a dull fool--a vain, drivelling, brainless idiot? Widow. No, no. Mel. What am I then--worse than all these? Why, I am a peasant! What has a peasant to do with love? Vain revolutions, why lavish your cruelty on the great? Oh that we--we, the hewers of wood and drawers of water--had been swept away, so that the proud might learn what the world would be without us! [Knock at the door.

Enter Servant from the Inn.

Servant. A letter for Citizen Melnotte.

Mel. A letter! from her perhaps--who sent thee?

Servant. Why, Monsieur--I mean Citizen--Beauseant, who stops to dine at the Golden Lion, on his way to his chateau.

Mel. Beauseant!--[Reads].

"Young man, I know thy secret--thou lovest above thy station: if thou
hast wit, courage, and discretion, I can secure to thee the realization
of thy most sanguine hopes; and the sole condition I ask in return is,
that thou shalt be steadfast to thine own ends. I shall demand from thee
a solemn oath to marry her whom thou lovest; to bear her to thine home
on thy wedding night. I am serious--if thou wouldst learn more, lose
not a moment, but follow the bearer of this letter to thy friend and
patron,--CHARLES BEAUSEANT."

Mel. Can I believe my eyes? Are our own passions the sorcerers that
raise up for us spirits of good or evil? I will go instantly.

Widow. What is this, Claude?

Mel. "Marry her whom thou lovest,"--"bear her to thine own home."--
Oh, revenge and love; which of you is the stronger?--[Gazing on the
picture.] Sweet face, thou smilest on me from the canvas: weak fool that
I am, do I then love her still? No, it is the vision of my own romance
that I have worshipped: it is the reality to which I bring scorn for
scorn. Adieu, mother: I will return anon. My brain reels--the earth
swims before me.--[Looks again at the letter.] No, it is not a mockery;
I do not dream! [Exit.

ACT II.--SCENE I.

The Gardens of M. DESCHAPPELLEs' house at Lyons--the house seen at the back of the stage.

Enter BEAUSEANT and GLAVIS.

Beau. Well, what think you of my plot? Has it not succeeded to a miracle? The instant that I introduced his Highness the Prince of Como to the pompous mother and the scornful daughter, it was all over with them: he came--he saw--he conquered: and, though it is not many days since he arrived, they have already promised him the hand of Pauline.

Gla. It is lucky, though, that you told them his highness travelled incognito, for fear the Directory (who are not very fond of princes) should lay him by the heels; for he has a wonderful wish to keep up his rank, and scatters our gold about with as much coolness as if he were watering his own flower-pots.

Beau. True, he is damnably extravagant; I think the sly dog does it out of malice. How ever, it must be owned that he reflects credit on his loyal subjects, and makes a very pretty figure in his fine clothes, with my diamond snuff-box.

Gla. And my diamond ring! But do you think he will be firm to the last? I fancy I see symptoms of relenting: he will never keep up his rank, if he once let out his conscience.

Beau. His oath binds him! he cannot retract without being foresworn, and those low fellows are always superstitious! But, as it is, I tremble lest he be discovered: that bluff Colonel Damas (Madame Deschappelles' cousin) evidently suspects him: we must make haste and conclude the farce: I have thought of a plan to end it this very day.

Gla. This very day! Poor Pauline: her dream will be soon over.

Beau. Yes, this day they shall be married; this evening, according to his oath, he shall carry his bride to the Golden Lion, and then pomp, equipage, retinue, and title, all shall vanish at once; and her Highness the Princess shall find that she has refused the son of a Marquis, to marry the son of a gardener.--Oh, Pauline! once loved, now hated, yet still not relinquished, thou shalt drain the cup to the dregs,--thou shalt know what it is to be humbled!

Enter from the house, MELNOTTE, as the Prince of Como, leading in PAULINE; MADAME

DESCHAPPELLES, fanning herself; and COLONEL DAMAS.

[BEAUSEANT and GLAVIS bow respectfully, fully. PAULINE and MEL-NOTTE walk
apart.

Mme. Deschap. Good morning, gentlemen; really I am so fatigued with laughter; the dear Prince is so entertaining. What wit he has! Any one may see that he has spent his whole life in courts.

Damas. And what the deuce do you know about courts, cousin Deschappelles? You women regard men just as you buy books--you never care about what is in them, but how they are bound and lettered. 'Sdeath, I don't think you would even look at your Bible if it had not a title to it.

Mme. Deschap. How coarse you are, cousin Damas!--quite the manners of a barrack--you don't deserve to be one of our family; really we must drop your acquaintance when Pauline marries. I cannot patronize any relations that would discredit my future son-in-law, the Prince of Como.

Mel. [advancing]. These are beautiful gardens, madame, [BEAUSEANT and GLAVIS retire]--who planned them?

Mme. Deschap. A gardener named Melnotte, your highness--an honest man who knew his station. I can't say as much for his son--a presuming fellow, who,--ha! ha! actually wrote verses--such doggerel!--to my daughter.

Pauline. Yes, how you would have laughed at them, Prince! you, who write such beautiful verses!

Mel. This Melnotte must be a monstrous impudent person!

Damas. Is he good-looking?

Mme. Deschap. I never notice such canaille--an ugly, mean-looking clown, if I remember right.

Damas. Yet I heard your porter say he was wonderfully like his highness.

Mel. [taking snuff]. You are complimentary.

Mme. Deschap. For shame, cousin Damas!--like the Prince, indeed!

Pauline. Like you! Ah, mother, like our beautiful prince! I'll never speak to you again, cousin Damas.

Mel. [aside]. Humph!--rank is a great beautifier! I never passed for an Apollo while I was a peasant; if I am so handsome as a prince, what should I be as an emperor! [Aloud.] Monsieur Beauseant, will you honor me? [Offers snuff.

Beau. No, your highness; I have no small vices.

Mel. Nay, if it were a vice, you'd be sure to have it, Monsieur Beauseant.

Mme. Deschap. Ha! ha!--how very severe!--what wit!

Beau. [in a rage and aside]. Curse his impertinence!

Mme. Deschap. What a superb snuff-box! Pauline. And what a beautiful ring!

Mel. You like the box--a trifle--interesting perhaps from associations-- a present from Louis XIV. to my great-great grandmother. Honor me by--accepting it.

Beau. plucking him by the sleeve. How!--what the devil! My box--are you mad? It is worth five hundred louis.

Mel. [unheeding him, and turning to PAULINE]. And you like this ring? Ah, it has, indeed a lustre since your eyes have shone on it placing it on her finger. Henceforth hold me, sweet enchantress, the Slave of the Ring.

Gla. [pulling him]. Stay, stay--what are you about? My maiden aunt's legacy--a diamond of the first water. You shall be hanged for swindling, sir.

Mel. [pretending not to hear]. It is curious, this ring; it is the one with which my grandfather, the Doge of Venice, married the Adriatic!

(Madame and PAULINE examine the ring.) Mel. [to BEAUSEANT and GLA-VIS].
Fie, gentlemen! princes must be generous?--[Turns to DAMAS, who watches them closely.] These kind friends have my interest so much at heart, that they are as careful of my property as if it were their own!

Beau and Gla. [confusedly]. Ha! ha!--very good joke that!

[Appears to remonstrate with MELNOTTE in dumb show.

Damas. What's all that whispering? I am sure there is some juggle here: hang me, if I think he is an Italian after all. Gad, I'll try him.
Servitore umillissimo, Eccellenza.* (* Your Excellency's most humble servant.)

Mel. Hum--what does he mean, I wonder?

Damas. Godo di vedervi in buona salute.* (* I am glad to see you in good health.)

Mel. Hem--hem!

Damas. Fa bel tempo--the si dice di nuovo? * (* Fine weather. What news is there?)

Mel. Well, sir, what's all that gibberish?

Damas. Oh, oh!--only Italian, your highness!--The Prince of Como does not understand his own language!

Mel. Not as you pronounce it; who the deuce could?

Mme. Deschap. Ha! ha! cousin Damas, never pretend to what you don't know.

Pauline. Ha! ha! cousin Damas; you speak Italian, indeed!

[Makes a mocking gesture at him.

Beau. [to GLAVIS]. Clever dog!--how ready!

Gla. Ready, yes; with my diamond ring!--Damn his readiness!

Damas. Laugh at me!--laugh at a Colonel in the French army!--the fellow's an impostor; I know he is. I'll see if he understands fighting as well as he does Italian.--[Goes up to him, and aside.] Sir, you are a jackanapes.--Can you construe that?

Mel. No, sir; I never construe affronts in the presence of ladies; by-and-by I shall be happy to take a lesson--or give one.

Damas. I'll find the occasion, never fear!

Mme. Deschap. Where are you going, cousin?

Damas. To correct my Italian. [Exit.

Beau. [to GLAVIS]. Let us after, and pacify him; he evidently suspects something.

Gla. Yes!--but my diamond ring!

Beau. And my box!--We are over-taxed fellow-subjects!--we must stop the supplies, and dethrone the prince.

Gla. Prince!--he ought to be heir-apparent to King Stork.

[Exeunt BEAUSEANT and GLAVIS.

Mme. Deschap. Dare I ask your highness to forgive my cousin's insufferable vulgarity?

Pauline. Oh yes!--you will forgive his manner for the sake of his heart.

Mel. And the sake of his cousin.--Ah, madam, there is one comfort in rank,--we are so sure of our position that we are not easily affronted. Besides, M. Damas has bought the right of indulgence from his friends, by never showing it to his enemies.

Pauline. Ah! he is, indeed, as brave in action as he is rude in speech. He rose from the ranks to his present grade, and in two years!

Mel. In two years!--two years, did you say?

Mme. Deschap. [aside]. I don't like leaving girls alone with their lovers; but, with a prince, it would be so ill-bred to be prudish. [Exit.

Mel. You can be proud of your connection with one who owes his position to merit--not birth.

Pauline. Why, yes; but still

Mel. Still what, Pauline!

Pauline. There is something glorious in the heritage of command. A man who has ancestors is like a representative of the past.

Mel. True; but, like other representatives, nine times out of ten he is a silent member. Ah, Pauline! not to the past, but to the future, looks true nobility, and finds its blazon in posterity.

Pauline. You say this to please me, who have no ancestors; but you, prince, must be proud of so illustrious a race!

Mel. No, no! I would not, were I fifty times a prince, be a pensioner on the dead! I honor birth and ancestry when they are regarded as the incentives to exertion, not the titledeeds to sloth! I honor the laurels that overshadow the graves of our fathers; it is our fathers I emulate, when I desire that beneath the evergreen I myself have planted, my own ashes may repose! Dearest! couldst thou but see with my eyes!

Pauline. I cannot forego pride when I look on thee, and think that thou lovest me. Sweet Prince, tell me again of thy palace by the Lake of Como; it is so pleasant to hear of thy splendors since thou didst swear to me that they would be desolate without Pauline; and when thou describest them, it is with a mocking lip and a noble scorn, as if custom had made thee disdain greatness.

Mel. Nay, dearest, nay, if thou wouldst have me paint The home to which, could love fulfil its prayers, This hand would lead thee, listen!*--

(* The reader will observe that Melnotte evades the request of Pauline. He proceeds to describe a home, which he does not say he possesses, but to which he would lead her, "could Love fulfil its prayers." This caution is intended as a

reply to a sagacious critic who censures the description,
because it is not an exact and prosaic inventory of the
characteristics of the Lake of Como!--When Melnotte, for
instance, talks of birds "that syllable the name of Pauline"
(by the way, a literal translation from an Italian poet), he
is not thinking of ornithology, but probably of the Arabian
Nights. He is venting the extravagant, but natural,
enthusiasm of the poet and the lover.)

A deep vale
Shut out by Alphine hills from the rude world;
Near a clear lake, margin'd by fruits of gold
And whispering myrtles; glassing softest skies,
As cloudless, save with rare and roseate shadows,
As I would have thy fate!

Pauline. My own dear love!

Mel. A palace lifting to eternal summer
Its marble walls, from out a glossy bower
Of coolest foliage musical with birds,
Whose songs should syllable thy name! At noon
We'd sit beneath the arching vines, and wonder
Why Earth could be unhappy, while the Heavens
Still left us youth and love! We'd have no friends
That were not lovers; no ambition, save
To excel them all in love; we'd read no books
That were not tales of love--that we might smile
To think how poorly eloquence of words
Translates the poetry of hearts like ours!
And when night came, amidst the breathless Heavens
We'd guess what star should be our home when love
Becomes immortal; while the perfumed light

Stole through the mists of alabaster lamps,
And every air was heavy with the sighs
Of orange-groves and music from sweet lutes,
And murmurs of low fountains that gush forth
I' the midst of roses!--Dost thou like the picture?

Pauline. Oh, as the bee upon the flower, I hang
Upon the honey of thy eloquent tongue!
Am I not blest? And if I love too wildly,
Who would not love thee like Pauline?

Mel. [bitterly.] Oh, false one!
It is the prince thou lovest, not the man
If in the stead of luxury, pomp, and power,
I had painted poverty, and toil, and care,
Thou hadst found no honey on my tongue;--Pauline,
That is not love!

Pauline. Thou wrong'st me, cruel Prince!
At first, in truth, I might not have been won,
Save through the weakness of a flatter'd pride;
But now,--oh! trust me,--couldst thou fall from power
And sink--

Mel. As low as that poor gardener's son
Who dared to lift his eyes to thee?--

Pauline. Even then,
Methinks thou wouldst be only made more dear
By the sweet thought that I could prove how deep
Is woman's love! We are like the insects, caught
By the poor glittering of a garish flame;
But, oh, the wings once scorch'd, the brightest star

Lures us no more; and by the fatal light
We cling till death!

Mel. Angel! [Aside.] O conscience! conscience!
It must not be; her love hath grown a torture
Worse than her hate. I will at once to Beauseant,
And--ha! he comes. Sweet love, one moment leave me.
I have business with these gentlemen--I--I
Will forwith join you.

Pauline. Do not tarry long! [Exit.

Enter BEAUSEANT and GLAVIS.

Mel. Release me from my oath,--I will not marry her!

Beau Then thou art perjured.

Mel. No, I was not in my senses when I swore to thee to marry her! I
was blind to all but her scorn!--deaf to all but my passion and my rage!
Give me back my poverty and my honor!

Beau. It is too late,--you must marry her! and this day. I have a story
already coined, and sure to pass current. This Damas suspects thee,--he
will set the police to work!--thou wilt be detected--Pauline will
despise and execrate thee. Thou wilt be sent to the common gaol as a
swindler.

Mel. Fiend!

Beau. And in the heat of the girl's resentment (you know of what
resentment is capable) and the parents' shame, she will be induced to
marry the first that offers--even perhaps your humble servant.

Mel. You! No; that were worse--for thou hast no mercy! I will marry her.--I will keep my oath. Quick, then, with the damnable invention thou art hatching;--quick, if thou wouldst not have me strangle thee or myself.

Gla. What a tiger! Too fierce for a prince; he ought to have been the Grand Turk.

Beau. Enough--I will dispatch; be prepared.

[Exeunt BEAUSEANT and GLAVIS.

Enter DAMAS with two swords.

Damas. Now, then, sir, the ladies are no longer your excuse. I have brought you a couple of dictionaries; let us see if your highness can find out the Latin for bilbo.

Mel. Away, sir! I am in no humor for jesting. Damas. I see you understand something of the grammar; you decline the non-substantive "small-swords" with great ease; but that won't do--you must take a lesson in parsing.

Mel. Fool! Damas. Sir, as sons take after their mother, so the man who calls me a fool insults the lady who bore me; there's no escape for you--fight you shall, or--

Mel. Oh, enough! enough!--take your ground.

They fight; DAMAS is disarmed. MELNOTTE takes up the sword and returns it to DAMAS respectfully. A just punishment to the brave soldier who robs the state of its best property--the sole right to his valor and his life.

Damas. Sir, you fence exceedingly well; you must be a man of honor--I don't care a jot whether you are a prince; but a man who has carte and tierce at his fingers' ends must be a gentleman.

Mel. [aside.] Gentleman! Ay, I was a gentleman before I turned conspirator; for honest men are the gentlemen of Nature! Colonel, they tell me you rose from the ranks.

Damas. I did.

Mel. And in two years!

Damas. It is true; that's no wonder in our army at present. Why the oldest general in the service is scarcely thirty, and we have some of two-and-twenty.

Mel. Two-and-twenty!

Damas. Yes; in the French army, now a days, promotion is not a matter of purchase. We are all heroes, because we may be all generals. We have no fear of the cypress, because we may all hope for the laurel.

Mel. A general at two-and-twenty! [turning away]--Sir, I may ask you a favor one of these days.

Damas. Sir, I shall be proud to grant it. It is astonishing how much I like a man after I've fought with him. [Hides the swords.

Enter MADAME DESCHAPPELLES and BEAUSEANT.

Mme. Deschap. Oh, prince,--prince!--What do I hear? You must fly--you must quit us!

Mel. I!

Beau. Yes, prince: read this letter, just received from my friend at
Paris, one of the Directory; they suspect you of designs against the
Republic: they are very suspicious of princes, and your family take part
with the Austrians. Knowing that I introduced your highness at Lyons, my
friend writes to me to say that you must quit the town immediately, or
you will be arrested,--thrown into prison, perhaps guillotined! Fly!--I
will order horses to your carriage instantly. Fly to Marsailles; there
you can take ship to Leghorn.

Mme. Deschap. And what's to become of Pauline? Am I not to be mother to
a princess, after all?

Enter PAULINE and MONSIEUR DESCHAPPELLES.

Pauline [throwing herself into MELNOTTE's arms.] You must leave
us!--Leave Pauline!

Beau. Not a moment is to be wasted.

M. Deschap. I will go to the magistrates and inquire--

Beau. Then he is lost; the magistrates, hearing he is suspected, will
order his arrest.

Mme. Deschap. And I shall not be a princess-dowager!

Beau. Why not? There is only one thing to be done:--send for the
priest--let the marriage take place at once, and the prince carry home
a bride?

Mel. Impossible!--[Aside.] Villain.

Mme. Deschap. What, lose my child?

Beau. And gain a princess!

Mme Deschap. Oh, Monsieur Beauseant, you are so very kind, it must be so,--we ought not to be selfish, my daughter's happiness at stake. She will go away, too, in a carriage and six!

Pauline. Thou art here still,--I cannot part from my heart will break.

Mel. But thou wilt not consent to this hasty union?--thou wilt not wed an outcast--a fugitive?

Pauline. Ah! if thou art in danger, who should share it but Pauline?

Mel. [aside]. Distraction!--If the earth could swallow me!

M. Deschap. Gently! gently! The settlements--the contracts--my daughter's dowry!

Mel. The dowry!--I am not base enough for that; no, not one farthing!

Beau. [to MADAM]. Noble fellow!--Really your good husband is too mercantile in these matters. Monsieur Deschappelles, you hear his highness: we can arrange the settlements by proxy; 'tis the way with people of quality.

M. Deschap. But--

Mme. Deschap. Hold your tongue!--Don't expose yourself!

Beau. I will bring the priest in a trice. Go in all of you and prepare; the carriage shall be at the door before the ceremony is over.

Mme. Deschap. Be sure there are six horses, Beauseant! You are very good to have forgiven us for refusing you; but you see--a prince!

Beau. And such a prince! Madam, I cannot blush at the success of so illustrious a rival.--[Aside.] Now will I follow them to the village, enjoy my triumph, and to-morrow, in the hour of thy shame and grief, I think, proud girl, thou wilt prefer even these arms to those of the gardener's son. [Exit.

Mme. Deschap. Come, Monsieur Deschappelles, give your arm to her highness that is to be.

M. Deschap. I don't like doing business in such a hurry; 'tis not the way with the house of Deschappelles & Co.

Mme. Deschap. There, now, you fancy you are in the counting-house, don't you?

[Pushes him to PAULINE.

Mel. Stay, stay, Pauline--one word. Have you no scruple, no fear? Speak--it is not yet too late.

Pauline. When I loved thee, thy fate became mine. Triumph or danger-- joy or sorrow--I am by thy side.

Damas. Well, well, prince, thou art a lucky man to be so loved. She is a good little girl in spite of her foibles make her as happy as if she were not to be a princess [slapping him on the shoulder]. Come, sir, I wish you joy--young tender--lovely;--zounds, I envy you!

Mel. [who has stood apart in gloomy abstraction]. Do you?*

(* On the stage the following lines are added:--)

"Do you? Wise judges are we of each other.
'Woo, wed, and bear her home! So runs the bond
To which I sold myself,--and then--what then?
Away?--I will not look beyond the hour.
Like children in the dark, I dare not face
The shades that gather sound me in the distance.
You envy me--I thank you--you may read
My joy upon my brow--I thank you, sir!
If hearts had audible language, you would hear
What mine would answer when you talk of ENVY!"

ACT III.--SCENE I.

The exterior of the Golden Leon--time, twilight. The moon rises during the scene.

Enter Landlord and his Daughter from the Inn.

Land. Ha--ha--ha! Well, I never shall get over it. Our Claude is a prince with a vengeance now. His carriage breaks down at my inn--ha--ha!

Janet. And what airs the young lady gives herself! "Is this the best room you have, young woman?" with such a toss of the head.

Land. Well, get in, Janet: get in and see to the supper: the servants must sup before they go back. [Exeunt.

Enter BEAUSEANT and GLAVIS.

Beau. You see our princess is lodged at last--one stage more, and she'll be at her journey's end--the beautiful palace at the foot of the Alps!--ha--ha!

Gla. Faith, I pity the poor Pauline--especially if she's going to sup at the Golden Lion [makes a wry face]. I shall never forget that cursed ragout.

Enter MELNOTTE from the Inn.

Beau. Your servant, my prince; you reigned most worthily, I condole with you on your abdication. I am afraid that your highness's retinue are not very faithful servants. I think they will quit you in the moment of your fall 'tis the fate of greatness. But you are welcome to your fine clothes--also the diamond snuff-box, which Louis XIV. gave to your great-great-grandmother.

Gla. And the ring, with which your grandfather the Dodge of Venice married the Adriatic.

Mel. I have kept my oath, gentlemen--say, have I kept my oath?

Beau. Most religiously.

Mel. Then you have done with me and mine--away with you!

Beau. How, knave?

Mel. Look you, our bond is over. Proud conquerors that we are, we have won the victory over a simple girl compromised her honor--embittered her life--blasted, in their very blossoms, all the flowers of her youth. This is your triumph,--it is my shame! [Turns to BEAUSEANT.] Enjoy thy triumph, but not in my sight. I was her betrayer--I am her protector! Cross but her path--one word of scorn, one look of insult--nay, but one quiver of that mocking lip, and I will teach thee that bitter word thou hast graven eternally in this heart--Repentance.

Beau. His highness is most grandiloquent.

Mel. Highness me no more! Beware! Remorse has made me a new being. Away with you! There is danger in me. Away!

Gla. [aside]. He's an awkward fellow to deal with: come away, Beauseant.

Beau. I know the respect clue to rank. Adieu, my prince. Any commands at Lyons? Yet hold--I promised you 200 Louis on your wedding-day; here they are.

Mel. [dashing the purse to the ground]. I gave you revenge, I did not sell it. Take up your silver, Judas; take it. Ay, it is fit you should learn to stoop.

Beau. You will beg my pardon for this some clay. [Aside to GLAVIS.] Come to my chateau--I shall return hither to morrow, to learn how Pauline likes her new dignity.

Mel. Are you not gone yet?

Beau. Your highness's most obedient, most faithful

Gla. And most humble servants. Ha! ha! [Exeunt BEAUSEANT and GLAVIS.

Mel. Thank heaven I had no weapon, or I should have slain them. Wretch! what can I say? Where turn? On all sides mockery--the very boors within--[Laughter from the Inn].--'Sdeath, if even in this short absence the exposure should have chanced. I will call her. We will go hence. I have already sent one I can trust to my mother's house. There, at least, none can insult her agony--gloat upon her shame! There alone must she learn what a villain she has sworn to love. [As he turns to the door enter PAULINE from the Inn.

Pauline. Ah! my lord, what a place! I never saw such rude people. They stare and wink so. I think the very sight of a prince, though he travels incognito, turns their honest heads. What a pity the carriage should break down in such a spot! You are not well--the drops stand on your brow--your hand is feverish.

Mel. Nay, it is but a passing spasm;--the air

Pauline. Is not the soft air of your native south--How pale he
is!--indeed thou art not well. Where are our people? I will call them.

Mel. Hold! I--I am well.

> Pauline. Thou art!--Ah! now I know it.
> Thou fanciest, my kind lord--I know thou dost--
> Thou fanciest these rude walls, these rustic gossips,
> Brick'd floors, sour wine, coarse viands, vex Pauline;
> And so they might, but thou art by my side,
> And I forget all else.

Enter Landlord, the Servants peeping and laughing over his shoulder.

Land. My lord--your highness--Will your most noble excellency choose--

> Mel. Begone, sir! [Exit Landlord laughing.

> Pauline. How could they have learn'd thy rank?
> One's servants are so vain!--nay, let it not
> Chafe thee, sweet prince!--a few short days and we
> Shall see thy palace by its lake of silver,
> And--nay, nay, spendthrift, is thy wealth of smiles,
> Already drain'd, or dost thou play the miser?

> Mel. Thine eyes would call up smiles in deserts, fair one.
> Let us escape these rustics: close at hand
> There is a cot, where I have bid prepare
> Our evening lodgment--a rude, homely roof,

But honest, where our welcome will not be
Made torture by the vulgar eyes and tongues
That are as death to Love! A heavenly night!
The wooing air and the soft moon invite us.
Wilt walk? I pray thee, now,--I know the path,
Ay, every inch of it!

Pauline. What, thou! Methought
Thou wert a stranger in these parts? Ah, truant,
Some village beauty lured thee;--thou art now
Grown constant?

Mel. Trust me.

Pauline. Princes are so changeful!

Mel. Come, dearest, come.

Pauline. Shall I not call our people To light us?

Mel. Heaven will lend its stars for torches! It is not far.

Pauline. The night breeze chills me.

Mel. Nay, Let me thus mantle thee;--it is not cold.

Pauline. Never beneath thy smile!

Mel. [aside.] O Heaven! forgive me! [Exeunt

SCENE II.

MELNOTTE'S cottage--Widow bustling about--a table spread for supper.

Widow. So, I think that looks very neat. He sent me a line, so blotted that I can scarcely read it, to say he would be here almost immediately. She must have loved him well indeed to have forgotten his birth; for though he was introduced to her in disguise, he is too honorable not to have revealed to her the artifice, which her love only could forgive. Well, I do not wonder at it; for though my son is not a prince, he ought to be one, and that's almost as good, [Knock at the door.] Ah! here they are.

Enter MELNOTTE and PAULINE.

Widow. Oh, my boy--the pride of my heart!--welcome, welcome! I beg pardon, ma'am, but I do love him so!

Pauline. Good woman, I really--why prince, what is this?--does the old lady know you? Oh, I guess, you have done her some service. Another proof of your kind heart? is it not?

Mel. Of my kind heart, ay!

Pauline. So you know the prince?

Widow. Know him, madam?--Ah, I begin to fear it is you who know him not!

Pauline. Do you think she is mad? Can we stay here, my lord? I think there's something very wild about her.

Mel. Madam, I--no, I cannot tell her; my knees knock together: what a coward is a man who has lost his honor! Speak to her--speak to her [to his mother]--tell her that--O Heaven, that I were dead!

Pauline. How confused he looks!--this strange place?--this woman--what can it mean?--I half suspect--Who are you, madam!--who are you! can't you speak? are you struck dumb?

Widow. Claude, you have not deceived her?--Ah, shame upon you! I thought that, before you went to the altar, she was to have known all.

Pauline. All! what!--My blood freezes in my veins!

Widow. Poor lady!--dare I tell her, Claude? [MELNOTTE makes a sign of assent.] Know you not then, madam, that this young man is of poor though honest parents? Know you not that you are wedded to my son, Claude Melnotte?

Pauline. Your son! hold--hold! do not speak to me.--[Approaches MELNOTTE, and lays her hand on his arm.]--Is this a jest? is it? I know it is, only speak--one word--one look one smile. I cannot believe--I who loved thee so--I cannot believe that thou art such a--No, I will not wrong thee by a harsh word--Speak!

Mel. Leave us--have pity on her, on me: leave us.

Widow. Oh, Claude, that I should live to see thee bowed by shame! thee of whom I was so proud! [Exit by the staircase.

Pauline. Her son--her son!

Mel. Now, lady, hear me.

Pauline. Hear thee! Ay, speak--her son! have fiends a parent? speak, That thou mayst silence curses--speak!

Mel. No, curse me: Thy curse would blast me less than thy forgiveness.

    Pauline [laughing wildly].

"This is thy palace, where the perfumed light
Steals through the mist of alabaster lamps,
And every air is heavy with the sighs
Of orange-groves, and music from the sweet lutes,
And murmurs of low fountains, that gush forth
I' the midst of roses!" Dost thou like the picture?
This is my bridal home, and thou my bridegroom.
O fool--O dupe--O wretch!--I see it all
Thy by-word and the jeer of every tongue
In Lyons. Hast thou in thy heart one touch
Of human kindness? if thou hast, why, kill me,
And save thy wife from madness. No, it cannot
It cannot be: this is some horrid dream:
I shall wake soon.--[Touching him.] Art flesh art man? or but
The shadows seen in sleep? It is too real.
What have I done to thee? how sinn'd against thee,
That thou shouldst crush me thus?

Mel. Pauline, by pride
Angels have fallen ere thy time: by pride
That sole alloy of thy most lovely mould
The evil spirit of a bitter love,
And a revengeful heart, had power upon thee.
From my first years my soul was fill'd with thee:
I saw thee midst the flow'rs the lowly boy
Tended, unmark'd by thee--a spirit of bloom,
And joy, and freshness, as if Spring itself
Were made a living thing, and wore thy shape!
I saw thee, and the passionate heart of man
Enter'd the breast of the wild-dreaming boy.
And from that hour I grew--what to the last
I shall be--thine adorer! Well, this love
Vain, frantic, guilty, if thou wilt, became

A fountain of ambition and bright hope;
I thought of tales that by the winter hearth
Old gossips tell--how maidens sprung from kings
Have stoop'd from their high sphere; how love, like death
Levels all ranks, and lays the shepherd's crook
Beside the sceptre. Thus I made my home
In the soft palace of a fairy Future!
My father died; and I, the peasant-born,
Was my own lord. Then did I seek to rise
Out of the prison of my mean estate;
And, with such jewels as the exploring mind
Brings from the caves of knowledge, buy my ransom
From those twin gaolers of the daring heart
Low birth and iron fortune. Thy bright image
Glass'd in my soul, took all the hues of glory,
And lured me on to those inspiring toils
By which man masters men! For thee I grew
A midnight student o'er the dreams of sages.
For thee I sought to borrow from each grace,
And every muse, such attributes as lend
Ideal charms to love. I thought of thee,
And passion taught me poesy--of thee,
And on the painter's canvas grew the life
Of beauty! Art became the shadow
Of the dear starlight of thy haunting eyes
Men call'd me vain--some mad--I heeded not;
But still toil'd on--hoped on--for it was sweet,
If not to win, to feel more worthy thee?

Pauline. Has he a magic to exorcise hate!

Mel. At last, in one mad hour, I dared to pour
The thoughts that burst their channels into song,

And sent them to thee--such a tribute, lady,
As beauty rarely scorns, even from the meanest.
The name--appended by the burning heart
That long'd to show its idol what bright things
It had created--yea, the enthusiast's name,
That should have been thy triumph, was thy scorn!
That very hour--when passion, turn'd to wrath,
Resembled hatred most--when thy disdain
Made my whole soul a chaos--in that hour
The tempters found me a revengeful tool
For their revenge! Thou hadst trampled on the worm
It turn'd and stung thee!

Pauline. Love, sir, hath no sting.
What was the slight of a poor powerless girl
To the deep wrong of this most vile revenge?
Oh, how I loved this man!--a serf!--a slave!

Mel. Hold, lady! No, not slave! Despair is free!
I will not tell thee of the throes--the struggles
The anguish--the remorse: No, let it pass!
And let me come to such most poor atonement
Yet in my power. Pauline!

[Approaching her with great emotion, and about to take her hand.

Pauline. No, touch me not!
I know my fate. You are, by law, my tyrant;
And I--O Heaven!--a peasant's wife! I'll work
Toil--drudge--do what thou wilt--but touch me not;
Let my wrongs make me sacred!

Mel. Do not fear me.
Thou dost not know me, madam: at the altar
My vengeance ceased--my guilty oath expired!
Henceforth, no image of some marble saint,
Niched in cathedral aisles, is hallow'd more
From the rude hand of sacrilegious wrong.
I am thy husband--nay, thou need'st not shudder;
Here, at thy feet, I lay a husband's rights.
A marriage thus unholy--unfulfill'd--
A bond of fraud--is, by the laws of France,
Made void and null. To-night sleep--sleep in peace.
To-morrow, pure and virgin as this morn
I bore thee, bathed in blushes, from the shrine,
Thy father's arms shall take thee to thy home.
The law shall do thee justice, and restore
Thy right to bless another with thy love.
And when thou art happy, and hast half forgot
Him who so loved--so wrong'd thee, think at least
Heaven left some remnant of the angel still
In that poor peasant's nature!

Ho! my mother! [Enter Widow.

Conduct this lady--(she is not my wife;
She is our guest,--our honor'd guest, my mother)--
To the poor chamber, where the sleep of virtue,
Never, beneath my father's honest roof,
Ev'n villains dared to mar! Now, lady, now,
I think thou wilt believe me. Go, my mother!

Widow. She is not thy wife!

Mel. Hush, hush! for mercy's sake! Speak not, but go.

[Widow ascends the stairs; PAULINE follows weeping--turns to look back.

Mel. [sinking down]. All angels bless and guard her!

ACT IV.--SCENE I.

The cottage as before--MELNOTTE seated before a table--writing implements, etc.--(Day breaking.)

Mel. Hush, hush!--she sleeps at last!--thank Heaven, for a while she forgets even that I live! Her sobs, which have gone to my heart the whole, long, desolate night, have ceased!--all calm--all still! I will go now; I will send this letter to Pauline's father: when he arrives, I will place in his hands my own consent to the divorce, and then, O France! my country! accept among thy protectors, thy defenders--the peasant's Son! Our country is less proud than custom, and does not refuse the blood, the heart, the right hand of the poor man.

Enter Widow.

Widow. My son, thou hast acted ill; but sin brings its own punishment. In the hour of thy remorse, it is not for a mother to reproach thee.

Mel. What is past is past. There is a future left to all men, who have the virtue to repent, and the energy to atone. Thou shalt be proud of thy son yet. Meanwhile, remember this poor lady has been grievously injured. For the sake of thy son's conscience, respect, honor, bear with her. If she weep, console--if she chide, be silent. 'Tis but a little while more--I shall send an express fast as horse can speed to her father. Farewell! I shall return shortly.

Widow. It is the only course left to thee--thou wert led astray, but thou art not hardened. Thy heart is right still, as ever it was when, in thy most ambitious hopes thou wert never ashamed of thy poor mother.

Mel. Ashamed of thee; No, if I yet endure, yet live, yet hope,--it is only because I would not die till I have redeemed the noble heritage I have lost--the heritage I took unstained from thee and my dead father--a proud conscience and an honest name. I shall win them back yet--heaven bless you! [Exit.

Widow. My dear Claude! How my heart bleeds for him.

[PAULINE looks down from above, and after a pause descends

Pauline. Not here!--he spares me that pain at least: so far he is considerate--yet the place seems still more desolate without him. Oh, that I could hate him--the gardener's son!--and yet how nobly he--no--no--no I will not be so mean a thing as to forgive him!

Widow. Good morning, madam; I would have waited on you if I had known you were stirring.

Pauline. It is no matter, ma'am--your son's wife ought to wait on herself.

Widow. My son's wife--let not that thought vex you, madam--he tells me that you will have your divorce. And I hope I shall live to see him smile again. There are maidens in this village, young and fair, madam, who may yet console him.

Pauline. I dare say--they are very welcome--and when the divorce is got--he will marry again. I am sure I hope so. [Weeps.

Widow. He could have married the richest girl in the province, if he had pleased it; but his head was turned, poor child! he could think of nothing but you. [Weeps.

Pauline. Don't weep, mother.

Widow. Ah, he has behaved very ill, I know, but love is so headstrong in the young. Don't weep, madam.

Pauline. So, as you were saying--go on.

Widow. Oh, I cannot excuse him, ma'am--he was not in his right senses.

Pauline. But he always--always [sobbing] loved--loved me then?

Widow. He thought of nothing else. See here--he learnt to paint that he might take your likeness [uncovers the picture]. But that's all over now--I trust you have cured him of his folly;--but, dear heart, you have had no breakfast!

Pauline. I can't take anything--don't trouble yourself.

Widow. Nay, madam, be persuaded; a little coffee will refresh you. Our milk and eggs are excellent. I will get out Claude's coffee-cup--It is of real Sevres; he saved up all his money to buy it three years ago, because the name of Pauline was inscribed on it.

Pauline. Three years ago! Poor Claude!--Thank you; I think I will have some coffee. Oh! if he were but a poor gentleman, even a merchant: but a gardener's son--and what a home!--Oh no,--it is too dreadful!

They seat themselves at the table, BEAUSEANT opens the lattice and looks in.

Beau. So--so--the coast is clear! I saw Claude in the lane--I shall
have an excellent opportunity. [Shuts the lattice and knocks at the door.

Pauline. [starting]. Can it be my father?--he has not sent for--him
yet? No, he cannot be in such a hurry to get rid of me.

Widow. It is not time for your father to arrive yet; it must be some
neighbor.

Pauline. Don't admit any one.

[Widow opens the door, BEAUSEANT pushes her aside and enters. Ha!
Heavens! that hateful Beauseant! This is indeed bitter!

Beau. Good morning, madam! O widow, your son begs you will have the
goodness to go to him in the village he wants to speak to you on
particular business; you'll find him at the inn, or the grocer's shop,
or the baker's, or at some other friend's of your family--make haste.

Pauline. Don't leave me, mother!--don't leave me.

Beau. [with great respect]. Be not alarmed, madam. Believe me your
friend--your servant.

Pauline. Sir, I have no fear of you, even in this house! Go, madam, if
your son wishes it; I will not contradict his commands whilst, at least
he has still the right to be obeyed.

Widow. I don't understand this; however, I sha'n't be long gone. [Exit.

Pauline. Sir, I divine the object of your visit--you wish to exult
in the humiliation of one who humbled you. Be it so; I am prepared to
endure all--even your presence!

Beau. You mistake me, madam--Pauline, you mistake me! I come to lay my fortune at your feet. You must already be disenchanted with this impostor; these walls are not worthy to be hallowed by your beauty! Shall that form be clasped in the arms of a base-born peasant? Beloved, beautiful Pauline! fly with me--my carriage waits without--I will bear you to a home more meet for your reception. Wealth, luxury, station--all shall yet be yours. I forget your past disdain--I remember only your beauty and my unconquerable love!

Pauline. Sir! leave this house--it is humble: but a husband's roof, however lowly, is, in the eyes of God and man, the temple of a wife's honor! Know that I would rather starve--yes--with him who has betrayed me, than accept your lawful hand, even were you the prince whose name he bore.--Go.

Beau. What! is not your pride humbled yet?

Pauline. Sir, what was pride in prosperity in affliction becomes virtue.

Beau. Look round: these rugged floors--these homely walls--this wretched struggle of poverty for comfort--think of this! and contrast with such a picture the refinement, the luxury, the pomp, that the wealthiest gentleman of Lyons offers to the loveliest lady. Ah, hear me!

Pauline. Oh! my father!--why did I leave you?--why am I thus friendless? Sir, you see before you a betrayed, injured, miserable woman!--respect her anguish.

[MELNOTTE opens the door silently, and pauses at the threshold.

Beau. No! let me rather thus console it; let me snatch from those lips one breath of that fragrance which never should be wasted on the low churl thy husband.

Pauline. Help! Claude!--Claude!--Have I no protector?'

Beau. Be silent! [showing a pistol.] See, I do not come unprepared even for violence. I will brave all things--thy husband and all his race--for thy sake. Thus, then, I clasp thee!

Mel. [dashing him to the other end of the stage]. Pauline--look up, Pauline! thou art safe.

Beau. [levelling his pistol]. Dare you thus insult a man of my birth, ruffian?

Pauline. Oh, spare him--spare my husband!--Beauseant--Claude--no--no [faints].

Mel. Miserable trickster! shame upon you! brave devices to terrify a woman! Coward!--you tremble--you have outraged the laws--you know that your weapon is harmless--you have the courage of the mountebank, not the bravo!--Pauline, there is no danger.

Beau. I wish thou wert a gentleman--as it is, thou art beneath me.--Good day, and a happy honeymoon.--[Aside.] I will not die till I am avenged. [Exit.

> Mel. I hold her in these arms--the last embrace
> Never, ah never more, shall this dear head
> Be pillow'd on the heart that should have shelter'd
> And has betray'd!--Soft--soft! one kiss--poor wretch!
> No scorn on that pale lip forbids me now!
> One kiss--so ends all record of my crime!
> It is the seal upon the tomb of hope,
> By which, like some lost, sorrowing angel, sits
> Sad memory evermore; she breathes--she moves

She wakes to scorn, to hate, but not to shudder
Beneath the touch of my abhorred love.
Places her on a seat. There--we are strangers now!

Pauline. All gone--all calm
Is every thing a dream? thou art safe, unhurt
I do not love thee;--but--but I am woman,
And--and--no blood is spilt?

Mel. No, lady, no; My guilt hath not deserved so rich a blessing As even danger in thy cause.

Enter WIDOW.

Widow. My son, I have been everywhere in search of you; why did you send for me?

Mel. I did not send for you.

Widow. No! but I must tell you your express has returned.

Mel. So soon! impossible!

Widow. Yes, he met the lady's father and mother on the road; they were going into the country on a visit. Your messenger says that Monsieur Deschappelles turned almost white with anger when he read your letter. They will be here almost immediately. Oh, Claude, Claude! what will they do to you? How I tremble! Ah, madam! do not let them injure him--if you knew how he doated on you.

Pauline. Injure him! no, ma'am, be not afraid;--my father! how shall I meet him? how go back to Lyons? the scoff of the whole city! Cruel, cruel, Claude [in great agitation]. Sir, you have acted most treacherously.

Mel. I know it, madam.

Pauline [aside.] If he would but ask me to forgive him!--I never can forgive you, sir.

Mel. I never dared to hope it.

Pauline. But you are my husband now, and I have sworn to--to love you, sir.

Mel. That was under a false belief, madam; Heaven and the laws will release you from your vow.

Pauline. He will drive me mad! if he were but less proud--if he would but ask me to remain--hark, hark--I hear the wheels of the carriage--Sir--Claude, they are coming; have you no word to say ere it is loo late? Quick speak.

Mel. I can only congratulate you on your release. Behold your parents

Enter MONSIEUR and MADAME DESCHAPPELLES and COLONEL DAMAS.

M. Deschap. My child! my child!

Mme. Deschap. Oh, my poor Pauline!--what a villanous hovel this is! Old woman, get me a chair--I shall faint I certainly shall. What will the world say? Child, you have been a fool. A mother's heart is easily broken.

Damas. Ha, ha! most noble Prince--I am sorry to see a man of your quality in such a condition; I am afraid your highness will go to the

House of Correction.

Mel. Taunt on, sir; I spared you when you were unarmed--I am unarmed now. A man who has no excuse for crime is indeed defenceless!

Damas. There's something fine in the rascal, after all!

M. Deschap. Where is the impostor?--Are you thus shameless, traitor? Can you brave the presence of that girl's father?

Mel. Strike me, if it please you--you are her father.

Pauline. Sir--sir, for my sake; whatever his guilt, he has acted nobly in atonement.

Mme. Deschap. Nobly! Are you mad, girl? I have no patience with you-- to disgrace all your family thus! Nobly! Oh you abominable, hardened, pitiful, mean, ugly villain!

Damas. Ugly! Why he was beautiful yesterday!

Pauline. Madame, this is his roof, and he is my husband. Respect your daughter, or let blame fall alone on her.

Mme. Deschap. You--you--Oh, I'm choking.

M. Deschap. Sir, it were idle to waste reproach upon a conscience like yours--you renounce all pretensions to the person of this lady?

Mel. I do. [Gives a paper.] Here is my consent to a divorce--my full confession of the fraud which annuls the marriage. Your daughter has been foully wronged--I grant it, sir; but her own lips will tell you that, from the hour in which she crossed this threshold, I returned to my own station, and respected hers. Pure and inviolate, as when yestermorn you laid your hand upon her head, and blessed her, I yield her back to you. For myself--I deliver you for ever from my presence. An outcast and a criminal, I seek some distant land, where I may mourn my sin, and pray for your daughter's peace. Farewell--farewell to you all, for ever!

Willow. Claude, Claude, you will not leave your poor old mother? She does not disown you in your sorrow no, not even in your guilt. No divorce can separate a mother from her son.

Pauline. This poor widow teaches me my duty. No, mother,--no, for you are now my mother also!--nor should any law, human or divine, separate the wife from her husband's sorrows. Claude--Claude--all is forgotten forgiven--I am thine for ever!

Mme. Deschap. What do I hear?--Come away, or never see my face again.

M. Deschap. Pauline, we never betrayed you!--do you forsake us for him?

Pauline. [going back to her father]. Oh no--but you will forgive him too; we will live together--he shall be your son.

M. Deschap. Never! Cling to him and forsake your parents! His home shall be yours--his fortune yours--his fate yours: the wealth I have acquired by honest industry shall never enrich the dishonest man.

Pauline. And you would have a wife enjoy luxury while a husband toils! Claude, take me; thou canst not give me wealth, titles, station--but thou canst give me a true heart I will work for thee, tend thee, bear with thee, and never, never shall these lips reproach thee for the past.

Damas. I'll be hanged if I am not going to blubber!

Mel. This is the heaviest blow of all!--What a heart I have wronged!--
Do not fear me, sir; I am not all hardened--I will not rob her of a
holier love than mine. Pauline!--angel of love and mercy!--your memory
shall lead me back to virtue!--The husband of a being so beautiful in
her noble and sublime tenderness may be poor--may be low born;--(there
is no guilt in the decrees of providence!)--but he should be one who
can look thee in the face without a blush,--to whom thy love does not
bring remorse,--who can fold thee to his heart, and say,--"Here there is
no deceit!" I am not that man!

Damas. [aside to MELNOTTE]. Thou art a noble fellow, notwithstanding;
and wouldst make an excellent soldier. Serve in my regiment. I have had
a letter from the Directory--our young general takes the command of the
army in Italy,--I am to join him at Marseilles, I will depart this day,
if thou wilt go with me.

Mel. It is the favor I would have asked thee, if I dared. Place me
wherever a foe is most dreaded,--wherever France most needs a life!

Damas. There shall not be a forlorn hope without thee!

Mel. There is my hand!--mother, your blessing. I shall see you again,--a
better man than a prince,--a man who has bought the right to high
thoughts by brave deeds. And thou!--thou! so wildly worshipped, so
guiltily betrayed, all is not yet lost!--for thy memory, at least,
must be mine till death! If I live, the name of him thou hast once loved
shall not rest dishonored;--if I fall, amidst the carnage and the roar
of battle, my soul will fly back to thee, and love shall share with
death my last sigh!--More--more would I speak to thee!--to pray!--to
bless! But no; When I am less unworthy I will utter it to Heaven!--I
cannot trust myself to [turning to DESCHAPPELLES] Your pardon, sir; they

are my last words Farewell! [Exit.

Damas. I will go after him.--France will thank me for this.

Pauline [starting from her father's arms]. Claude!--Claude!--my husband!

M. Deschap. You have a father still!

ACT V.

Two years and a half from the date of Act IV.

SCENE I.

The Streets of Lyons.

Enter First, Second, and Third Officers.

First Officer. Well, here we are at Lyons, with gallant old Damas: it is his native place.

Second Officer. Yes; he has gained a step in the army since he was here last. The Lyonnese ought to be very proud of stout General Damas.

Third Officer. Promotion is quick in the French army. This mysterious Morier,--the hero of Lodi, and the favorite of the commander-in-chief,--has risen to a colonel's rank to two years and a half. Enter DAMAS, as a General.

Damas. Good morrow, gentlemen; I hope you will amuse yourselves during our short stay at Lyons. It is a fine city: improved since I left it.
Ah! it is a pleasure to grow old, when the years that bring decay to

ourselves do but ripen the prosperity of our country. You have not met with Morier?

First Officer. No: we were just speaking of him.

Second Officer. Pray, general, can you tell us who this Morier really is?

Damas. Is!--why a colonel in the French army.

Third Officer. True. But what was he at first?

Damas. At first? Why a baby in long clothes, I suppose.

First Officer. Ha, ha! Ever facetious, general.

Second Officer. [to Third]. The general is sore upon this point; you will only chafe him.--Any commands, general?

Damas. None. Good day to you. [Exeunt Second and Third Officers.

Damas. Our comrades are very inquisitive. Poor Morier is the subject of a vast deal of curiosity.

First Officer. Say interest, rather, general. His constant melancholy, the loneliness of his habits,--his daring valor, his brilliant rise in the profession,--your friendship, and the favors of the commander-in-chief,--all tend to make him as much the matter of gossip as of admiration. But where is he, general? I have missed him all the morning.

Damas. Why, captain, I'll let you into a secret. My young friend has come with me to Lyons in hopes of finding a miracle.

First Officer. A miracle!

Damas. Yes, a miracle! in other words,--a constant woman.

First Officer. Oh! an affair of love!

Damas. Exactly so. No sooner did he enter Lyons than he waved his hand to me, threw himself from his horse, and is now, I warrant, asking every one who can know anything about the matter, whether a certain lady is still true to a certain gentleman!

First Officer. Success to him! and of that success there can be no doubt. The gallant Colonel Morier, the hero of Lodi, might make his choice out of the proudest families in France.

Damas. Oh, if pride be a recommendation, the lady and her mother are most handsomely endowed. By the way, captain, if you should chance to meet with Morier, tell him he will find me at the hotel.

First Officer. I will, general. [Exit.

Damas. Now will I go to the Deschappelles, and make a report to my young Colonel. Ha! by Mars, Bacchus, Apollo, Virorum,--here comes Monsieur Beauseant!

Enter BEAUSEANT.

Good morrow, Monsieur Beauseant! How fares it with you?

Beau. [aside.] Damas! that is unfortunate;--if the Italian campaign should have filled his pockets, he may seek to baffle me in the moment of my victory. [Aloud]. Your servant, general,--for such, I think, is your new distinction! Just arrived in Lyons?

Damas. Not an hour ago. Well, how go on the Deschappelles? Have they forgiven you in that affair of young Melnotte? You had some hand in that notable device,--eh?

Beau. Why, less than you think for! The fellow imposed upon me. I have set it all right now. What has become of him? He could not have joined the army, after all. There is no such name in the books.

Damas. I know nothing about Melnotte. As you say, I never heard the name in the Grand Army.

Beau. Hem!--You are not married, general?

Damas. Do I look like a married man, sir?--No, thank Heaven! My profession is to make widows, not wives.

Beau. You must have gained much booty in Italy! Pauline will be your heiress--eh?

Damas. Booty! Not I! Heiress to what? Two trunks and a portmanteau,-- four horses,--three swords, two suits of regimentals, and six pair of white leather inexpressibles! A pretty fortune for a young lady!

Beau. [aside.] Then all is safe! [Aloud]. Ha! ha! Is that really all your capital, General Damas? Why, I thought Italy had been a second Mexico to you soldiers.

Damas. All a toss-up, sir. I was not one of the lucky ones! My friend Morier, indeed, saved something handsome. But our commander-in-chief took care of him, and Morier is a thrifty, economical dog,--not like the rest of us soldiers, who spend our money as carelessly as if it were our blood.

Beau. Well, it is no matter! I do not want fortune with Pauline. And you must know, General Damas, that your fair cousin has at length consented to reward my long and ardent attachment.

Damas. You!--the devil! Why, she is already married! There is no divorce!

Beau. True; but this very day she is formally to authorize the necessary proceedings, this very day she is to sign the contract that is to make her mine within one week from the day on which her present illegal marriage is annulled.

Damas. You tell me wonders!--Wonders! No; I believe anything of women!

Beau. I must wish you good morning. [As he is going, enter DESCHAPPELLES.

M. Deschap. Oh, Beauseant! well met. Let us come to the notary at once.

Damas [to Deschap.]. Why, cousin!

M. Deschap. Damas, welcome to Lyons. Pray call on us; my wife will be delighted to see you.

Damas. Your wife be-blessed for her condescension! But [taking him aside] what do I hear? Is it possible that your daughter has consented to a divorce?--that she will marry Monsieur Beauseant?

M. Deschap. Certainly. What have you to say against it? A gentleman of birth, fortune, character. We are not so proud as we were; even my wife has had enough of nobility and princes!

Damas. But Pauline loved that young man so tenderly!

M. Deschap. [taking snuff]. That was two years and a half ago.

Damas. Very true. Poor Melnotte!

M. Deschap. But do not talk of that impostor; I hope he is dead or has left the country. Nay, even were he in Lyons at this moment, he ought to rejoice that, in an honorable and suitable alliance, my daughter may forget her sufferings and his crime.

Damas.--Nay, if it be all settled, I have no more to say. Monsieur Beauseant informs me that the contract is to be signed this very day.

M. Deschap, It is; at one o'clock precisely. Will you be one of the witnesses?

Damas. I?--No; that is to say--yes, certainly!--at one o'clock I will wait on you.

M. Deschap. Till then, adieu--come Beauseant.

[Exeunt BEAUSEANT and DESCHAPELLES

    Damas. The man who sets his heart upon a woman
    Is a chameleon, and doth feed on air;
    From air he takes his colors--holds his life,--
    Changes with every wind,--grows lean or fat,
    Rosy with hope, or green with jealousy,
    Or pallid with despair--just as the gale
    Varies from North to South--from heat to cold!
    Oh, woman! woman! thou shouldst have few sins
    Of thine own to answer for! Thou art the author
    Of such a book of follies in a man,
    That it would need the tears of all the angels

To blot the record out!

[Enter MELNOTTE, pale and agitated.

I need not tell thee! Thou hast heard--

Mel. The worst! I have!

Damas. Be cheer'd; others are fair as she is!

> Mel. Others! The world is crumbled at my feet!
> She was my world; fill'd up the whole of being--
> Smiled in the sunshine--walk'd the glorious earth--
> Sate in my heart--was the sweet life of life.
> The Past was hers; I dreamt not of a Future
> That did not wear her shape! Mem'ry and Hope
> Alike are gone. Pauline is faithless! Henceforth
> The universal space is desolate!

Damas. Hope yet.

> Mel. Hope, yes!--one hope is left me still--
> A soldier's grave! Glory has died with love.
> I look into my heart, and, where I saw
> Pauline, see Death!
>
> [After a pause].--But am I not deceived?
> I went but by the rumor of the town;
> Rumor is false,--I was too hasty! Damas,
> Whom hast thou seen?

Damas. Thy rival and her father. Arm thyself for the truth.--He heeds not.

Mel. She.

Will never know how deeply she was loved!
The charitable night, that wont to bring
Comfort to-day, in bright and eloquent dreams,
Is henceforth leagued with misery! Sleep, farewell,
Or else become eternal! Oh, the waking
From false oblivion, and to see the sun,
And know she is another's!

Damas. Be a man!

Mel. I am a man!--it is the sting of woe
Like mine that tells us we are men!

Damas. The false one
Did not deserve thee.

Mel. Hush!--No word against her!
Why should she keep, through years and silent absence,
The holy tablets of her virgin faith
True to a traitor's name! Oh, blame her not;
It were a sharper grief to think her worthless
Than to be what I am! To-day,--to-day!
They, said "To-day!" This day, so wildly welcomed--
This clay, my soul had singled out of time
And mark'd for bliss! This day! oh, could I see her,
See her once more unknown; but hear her voice.
So that one echo of its music might
Make ruin less appalling in its silence.

Damas. Easily done! Come with me to her house;
Your dress--your cloak--moustache--the bronzed hues

Of time and toil--the name you bear--belief
In your absence, all will ward away suspicion.
Keep in the shade. Ay, I would have you come
There may be hope? Pauline is yet so young,
They may have forced her to these second bridals
Out of mistaken love.

Mel. No, bid me hope not!
Bid me not hope! I could not bear again
To fall from such a heaven! One gleam of sunshine,
And the ice breaks and I am lost! Oh, Damas,
There's no such thing as courage in a man;
The veriest slave that ever crawl'd from danger
Might spurn me now. When first I lost her, Damas,
I bore it, did I not? I still had hope,
And now I--I-- [Bursts into an agony of grief.

Damas. What, comrade! all the women
That ever smiled destruction on brave hearts
Were not worth tears like these!

Mel. 'Tis past--forget it.
I am prepared; life has no further ills!
The cloud has broken in that stormy rain,
And on the waste I stand, alone with Heaven.

Damas. His very face is changed; a breaking heart
Does its work soon!--Come, Melnotte, rouse thyself:
One effort more. Again thou'lt see her.

Mel. See her!
There is a passion in that simple sentence
That shivers all the pride and power of reason

Into a chaos!

Damas. Time wanes; come, ere yet It be too late.

Mel. Terrible words--"Too late!" Lead on. One last look more, and then--

Damas. Forget her!

Mel. Forget her! yes--For death remembers not. [Exeunt.

SCENE II.

A room in the house of MONSIEUR DESCHAPPELLES; PAULINE seated in great dejection.

Pauline. It is so, then. I must be false to Love,
Or sacrifice a father! Oh, my Claude,
My lover, and my husband! Have I lived
To pray that thou mayest find some fairer boon
Than the deep faith of this devoted heart--
Nourish'd till now--now broken?

Enter MONSIEUR DESCHAPPELLES.

M. Deschap. My dear child,
How shall I thank--how bless thee? Thou hast saved,
I will not say my fortune--I could bear
Reverse, and shrink not--but that prouder wealth
Which merchants value most--my name, my credit--
The hard--won honors of a toilsome life:--
These thou hast saved, my child!

Pauline. Is there no hope?
No hope but this?

M. Deschap. None. If, without the sum
Which Beauseant offers for thy hand, this day
Sinks to the west--to-morrow brings our ruin!
And hundreds, mingled in that ruin, curse
The bankrupt merchant! and the insolvent herd
We feasted and made merry cry in scorn,
"How pride has fallen!--Lo, the bankrupt merchant!"
My daughter, thou hast saved us!

Pauline. And am lost!

M. Deschap. Come, let me hope that Beauseant's love--

Pauline. His love!
Talk not of love. Love has no thought of self!
Love buys not with the ruthless usurer's gold
The loathsome prostitution of a hand
Without a heart? Love sacrifices all things
To bless the thing it loves! He knows not love.
Father, his love is hate--his hope revenge!
My tears, my anguish, my remorse for falsehood--
These are the joys that he wrings from our despair!

M. Deschap. If thou deem'st thus, reject him! Shame and ruin
Were better than thy misery;--think no more on't.
My sand is wellnigh run--what boots it when
The glass is broken? We'll annul the contract:
And if to-morrow in the prisoner's cell
These aged limbs are laid, why still, my child,
I'll think thou art spared; and wait the Liberal Hour

That lays the beggar by the side of kings!

Pauline, No--no--forgive me! You, my honor'd father,--
You, who so loved, so cherish'd me, whose lips
Never knew one harsh word! I'm not ungrateful;
I am but human!--hush! Now, call the bridegroom--
You see I am prepared--no tears--all calm;
But, father, talk no more of love

M. Deschap. My child,
Tis but one struggle; he is young, rich, noble;
Thy state will rank first 'mid the dames of Lyons;
And when this heart can shelter thee no more,
Thy youth will not be guardianless.

Pauline. I have set
My foot upon the ploughshare--I will pass
The fiery ordeal. [Aside.] Merciful Heaven, support me;
And on the absent wanderer shed the light
Of happier stars--lost evermore to me!

Enter MADAME DESCHAPPELLES, BEAUSEANT, GLAVIS, and Notary.

Mme. Deschap. Why, Pauline, you are quite in deshabille--you ought to
be more alive to the importance of this joyful occasion. We had once
looked higher, it is true; but you see, after all, Monsieur Beauseant's
father was a Marquis, and that's a great comfort. Pedigree and
jointure!--you have them both in Monsieur Beauseant. A young lady
decorously brought up should only have two considerations in her choice
of a husband; first, is his birth honorable? secondly, will his death
be advantageous? All other trifling details should be left to parental
anxiety.

Beau. [approaching and waving aside Madame]. Ah, Pauline! let me hope
that you are reconciled to an event which confers such rapture upon me.

Pauline. I am reconciled to my doom.

Beau. Doom is a harsh word, sweet lady.

Pauline [aside.] This man must have some mercy--his heart cannot be
marble. [Aloud.] Oh, sir, be just--be generous! Seize a noble triumph--a
great revenge! Save the father, and spare the child.

Beau. [aside.] joy--joy alike to my hatred and my passion! The haughty
Pauline is at last my suppliant. [Aloud.] You ask from me what I
have not the sublime virtue to grant--a virtue reserved only for
the gardener's son! I cannot forego my hopes in the moment of their
fulfilment! I adhere to the contract--your father's ruin or your hand.

Pauline. Then all is over. Sir, I have decided.

[The clock strikes one.

Enter DAMAS and MELNOTTE.

Damas. Your servant, cousin Deschappelles. Let me introduce Colonel
Morier.

Mme. Deschap. [curtsying very low]. What, the celebrated hero? This is,
indeed, an honor! [MELNOTTE bows, and remains in the background.

Damas [to Pauline]. My little cousin, I congratulate you. What, no
smile--no blush? You are going to be divorced from poor Melnotte, and
marry this rich gentleman. You ought to be excessively happy!

Pauline. Happy!

Damas. Why, how pale you are, child!--Poor Pauline! Hist--confide in me!
Do they force you to this?

Pauline. No!

Damas. You act with your own free consent?

Pauline. My own consent--yes.

Damas. Then you are the most--I will not say what you are.

Pauline. You think ill of me--be it so--yet if you knew all--

Damas. There is some mystery--speak out, Pauline.

Pauline [suddenly]. Oh, perhaps you can save me! you are our
relation--our friend. My father is on the verge of bankruptcy--this day
he requires a large sum to meet demands that cannot be denied; that sum
Beauseant will advance--this hand the condition of the barter. Save me
if you have the means--save me! You will be repaid above!

Damas. aside. I recant--Women are not so bad after all! [Aloud.] Humph,
child! I cannot help you--I am too poor.

Pauline. The last plank to which I clung is shivered.

Damas. Hold--you see my friend Morier: Melnotte is his most intimate
friend--fought in the same fields--slept in the same tent. Have you any
message to send to Melnotte? any word to soften this blow?

Pauline. He knows Melnotte--he will see him--he will bear to him my last farewell--[approaches MELNOTTE] He has a stern air--he turns away from me--he despises me!--Sir one word I beseech you.

Mel. Her voice again! How the old time comes o'er me!

Damas [to Madame.] Don't interrupt them.--He is going to tell her what a rascal young Melnotte is; he knows him well, I promise you.

Mme. Deschap. So considerate in you, cousin Damas!

[DAMAS approaches DESCHAPPELLES; converses apart with hint in dumb show--DESCHAPPELLES shows him a paper, which he inspects and takes.

Pauline. Thrice have I sought to speak; my courage fails me.--
Sir, is it true that you have known--nay, are
The friend of--Melnotte.

Mel. Lady, yes!--
Myself And misery know the man!

Pauline. And you will see him,
And you will bear to him--ay--word for word,
All that this heart, which breaks in parting from him,
Would send, ere still for ever?

Mel. He hath told me
You have the right to choose from out the world
A worthier bridegroom;--he forgoes all claim,
Even to murmur at his doom. Speak on!

Pauline. Tell him, for years I never nursed a thought
That was not his;--that on his wandering way,

Daily and nightly, pour'd a mourner's prayers.
Tell him ev'n now that I would rather share
His lowliest lot,--walk by his side, an outcast--
Work for him, beg with him,--live upon the light
Of one kind smile from him,--than wear the crown
The Bourbon lost!

Mel. [aside.] Am I already mad?
And does delirium utter such sweet words
Into a dreamer's ear? [Aloud]. You love him thus,
And yet desert him?

Pauline. Say, that, if his eye--
Could read this heart,--its struggles, its temptations,--
His love itself would pardon that desertion!
Look on that poor old man,--he is my father;
He stands upon the verge of an abyss!--
He calls his child to save him! Shall I shrink
From him who gave me birth?--withhold my hand,
And see a parent perish? Tell him this,
And say--that we shall meet again in Heaven!

Mel. Lady--I--I--what is this riddle?--what
The nature of this sacrifice?

Pauline [pointing to DAMAS]. Go, ask him!

Beau. [from the table]. The papers are prepared--we only need
Your hand and seal.

Mel. Stay, lady--one word more.
Were but your duty with your faith united,
Would you still share the low-born peasant's lot?

Pauline. Would I? Ah, better death with him I love
Than all the pomp--which is but as the flowers
That crown the victim!--[Turning away.] I am ready.

[MELNOTTE rushes to DAMAS.

Damas. There--This is the schedule--this the total.

Beau. [to DESCHAPPELLES, showing notes]. These
Are yours the instant she has sign'd; you are
Still the great House of Lyons!

[The Notary is about to hand the contract to PAULINE, when MELNOTTE
seizes it and tears it.

Beau. Are you mad?

M. Deschap. How, Sir! What means this insult?

Mel. Peace, old man!
I have a prior claim. Before the face
Of man and Heaven I urge it; I outbid
Yon sordid huckster for your priceless jewel. [Giving a pocket-book.
There is the sum twice told! Blush not to take it:
There's not a coin that is not bought and hallow'd
In the cause of nations with a soldier's blood!

Beau. Torments and death!

Pauline. That voice! Thou art--

Mel. Thy husband!

[PAULINE rushes into his arms.

Look up! Look up, Pauline!--for I can bear
Thine eyes! The stain is blotted from my name.
I have redeem'd mine honor. I can call
On France to sanction thy divine forgiveness!
Oh, joy!--Oh, rapture! By the midnight watchfires
Thus have I seen thee! thus foretold this hour!
And 'midst the roar of battle, thus have heard
The beating of thy heart against my own!

Beau. Fool'd, duped, and triumph'd over in the hour
Of mine own victory! Curses on ye both!
May thorns be planted in the marriage-bed!
And love grow sour'd and blacken'd into hate
Such as the hate that gnaws me!

Damas. Curse away
And let me tell thee, Beauseant, a wise proverb
The Arabs have,--"Curses are like young chickens,
[Solemnly.] And still come home to roost!"

Beau. Their happiness
Maddens my soul! I am powerless and revengeless! [To MADAME.
I wish you joy! Ha! ha! the gardener's son! [Exit.

Damas [to GLAVIS]. Your friend intends to hang himself! Methinks
You ought to be his travelling companion!

Gla. Sir, you are exceedingly obliging! [Exit.

Pauline. Oh
My father, you are saved,--and by my husband!

Ah, blessed hour!

Mel. Yet you weep still, Pauline.

Pauline. But on thy breast!--these tears are sweet and holy!

M. Deschap. You have won love and honor nobly, sir!
Take her;--be happy both!

Mme. Deschap. I'm all astonish'd!
Who, then, is Colonel Morier?

Damas. You behold him!

Mel. Morier no more after this happy day!
I would not bear again my father's name
Till I could deem it spotless! The hour's come!
Heaven smiled on conscience! As the soldier rose
From rank to rank, how sacred was the fame
That cancell'd crime, and raised him nearer thee!

Mme. Deschap. A Colonel and a hero! Well, that's something!
He's wondrously improved! I wish you joy, sir!

Mel. Ah! the same love that tempts us into sin,
If it be true love, works out its redemption;
And he who seeks repentance for the Past
Should woo the Angel Virtue in the Future.

The Codes Of Hammurabi And Moses
W. W. Davies

QTY

The discovery of the Hammurabi Code is one of the greatest achievements of archaeology, and is of paramount interest, not only to the student of the Bible, but also to all those interested in ancient history...

Religion   ISBN: *1-59462-338-4*   **Pages:132**

MSRP $12.95

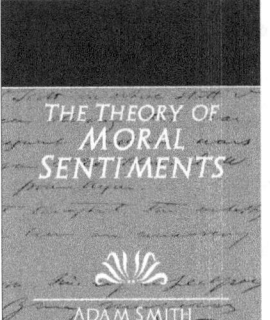

The Theory of Moral Sentiments
Adam Smith

QTY

This work from 1749. contains original theories of conscience amd moral judgment and it is the foundation for systemof morals.

Philosophy ISBN: *1-59462-777-0*   **Pages:536**

MSRP $19.95

Jessica's First Prayer
Hesba Stretton

QTY

In a screened and secluded corner of one of the many railway-bridges which span the streets of London there could be seen a few years ago, from five o'clock every morning until half past eight, a tidily set-out coffee-stall, consisting of a trestle and board, upon which stood two large tin cans, with a small fire of charcoal burning under each so as to keep the coffee boiling during the early hours of the morning when the work-people were thronging into the city on their way to their daily toil...

Childrens   ISBN: *1-59462-373-2*   **Pages:84**

MSRP $9.95

My Life and Work
Henry Ford

QTY

Henry Ford revolutionized the world with his implementation of mass production for the Model T automobile. Gain valuable business insight into his life and work with his own auto-biography... "We have only started on our development of our country we have not as yet, with all our talk of wonderful progress, done more than scratch the surface. The progress has been wonderful enough but..."

Biographies/   ISBN: *1-59462-198-5*   **Pages:300**

MSRP $21.95

www.bookjungle.com *email: sales@bookjungle.com fax: 630-214-0564 mail: Book Jungle PO Box 2226 Champaign, IL 61825*

The Art of Cross-Examination
Francis Wellman

QTY

I presume it is the experience of every author, after his first book is published upon an important subject, to be almost overwhelmed with a wealth of ideas and illustrations which could readily have been included in his book, and which to his own mind, at least, seem to make a second edition inevitable. Such certainly was the case with me; and when the first edition had reached its sixth impression in five months, I rejoiced to learn that it seemed to my publishers that the book had met with a sufficiently favorable reception to justify a second and considerably enlarged edition. ..

Pages:412

Reference   ISBN: *1-59462-647-2*   *MSRP $19.95*

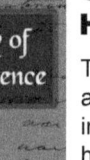

On the Duty of Civil Disobedience
Henry David Thoreau

QTY

Thoreau wrote his famous essay, On the Duty of Civil Disobedience, as a protest against an unjust but popular war and the immoral but popular institution of slave-owning. He did more than write—he declined to pay his taxes, and was hauled off to gaol in consequence. Who can say how much this refusal of his hastened the end of the war and of slavery ?

Law   **ISBN:** *1-59462-747-9*   **Pages:48**

MSRP $7.45

Dream Psychology Psychoanalysis for Beginners
Sigmund Freud

QTY

Sigmund Freud, born Sigismund Schlomo Freud (May 6, 1856 - September 23, 1939), was a Jewish-Austrian neurologist and psychiatrist who co-founded the psychoanalytic school of psychology. Freud is best known for his theories of the unconscious mind, especially involving the mechanism of repression; his redefinition of sexual desire as mobile and directed towards a wide variety of objects; and his therapeutic techniques, especially his understanding of transference in the therapeutic relationship and the presumed value of dreams as sources of insight into unconscious desires.

Pages:196

Psychology   ISBN: *1-59462-905-6*   *MSRP $15.45*

Dream Psychology
Psychoanalysis for Beginners

Sigmund Freud

The Miracle of Right Thought
Orison Swett Marden

QTY

Believe with all of your heart that you will do what you were made to do. When the mind has once formed the habit of holding cheerful, happy, prosperous pictures, it will not be easy to form the opposite habit. It does not matter how improbable or how far away this realization may see, or how dark the prospects may be, if we visualize them as best we can, as vividly as possible, hold tenaciously to them and vigorously struggle to attain them, they will gradually become actualized, realized in the life. But a desire, a longing without endeavor, a yearning abandoned or held indifferently will vanish without realization.

Pages:360

Self Help   ISBN: *1-59462-644-8*   *MSRP $25.45*

QTY

The Rosicrucian Cosmo-Conception Mystic Christianity *by Max Heindel* ISBN: *1-59462-188-8* **$38.95**
The Rosicrucian Cosmo-conception is not dogmatic, neither does it appeal to any other authority than the reason of the student. It is: not controversial, but is: sent forth in the, hope that it may help to clear... New Age/Religion Pages 646

Abandonment To Divine Providence *by Jean-Pierre de Caussade* ISBN: *1-59462-228-0* **$25.95**
"The Rev. Jean Pierre de Caussade was one of the most remarkable spiritual writers of the Society of Jesus in France in the 18th Century. His death took place at Toulouse in 1751. His works have gone through many editions and have been republished... Inspirational/Religion Pages 400

Mental Chemistry *by Charles Haanel* ISBN: *1-59462-192-6* **$23.95**
Mental Chemistry allows the change of material conditions by combining and appropriately utilizing the power of the mind. Much like applied chemistry creates something new and unique out of careful combinations of chemicals the mastery of mental chemistry... New Age Pages 354

The Letters of Robert Browning and Elizabeth Barret Barrett 1845-1846 vol II ISBN: *1-59462-193-4* **$35.95**
by Robert Browning and Elizabeth Barrett Biographies Pages 596

Gleanings In Genesis (volume I) *by Arthur W. Pink* ISBN: *1-59462-130-6* **$27.45**
Appropriately has Genesis been termed "the seed plot of the Bible" for in it we have, in germ form, almost all of the great doctrines which are afterwards fully developed in the books of Scripture which follow... Religion/Inspirational Pages 420

The Master Key *by L. W. de Laurence* ISBN: *1-59462-001-6* **$30.95**
In no branch of human knowledge has there been a more lively increase of the spirit of research during the past few years than in the study of Psychology, Concentration and Mental Discipline. The requests for authentic lessons in Thought Control, Mental Discipline and... New Age/Business Pages 422

The Lesser Key Of Solomon Goetia *by L. W. de Laurence* ISBN: *1-59462-092-X* **$9.95**
This translation of the first book of the "Lernegton" which is now for the first time made accessible to students of Talismanic Magic was done, after careful collation and edition, from numerous Ancient Manuscripts in Hebrew, Latin, and French... New Age/Occult Pages 92

Rubaiyat Of Omar Khayyam *by Edward Fitzgerald* ISBN:*1-59462-332-5* **$13.95**
Edward Fitzgerald, whom the world has already learned, in spite of his own efforts to remain within the shadow of anonymity, to look upon as one of the rarest poets of the century, was born at Bredfield, in Suffolk, on the 31st of March, 1809. He was the third son of John Purcell... Music Pages 172

Ancient Law *by Henry Maine* ISBN: *1-59462-128-4* **$29.95**
The chief object of the following pages is to indicate some of the earliest ideas of mankind, as they are reflected in Ancient Law, and to point out the relation of those ideas to modern thought. Religiom/History Pages 452

Far-Away Stories *by William J. Locke* ISBN: *1-59462-129-2* **$19.45**
"Good wine needs no bush, but a collection of mixed vintages does. And this book is just such a collection. Some of the stories I do not want to remain buried for ever in the museum files of dead magazine-numbers an author's not unpardonable vanity..." Fiction Pages 272

Life of David Crockett *by David Crockett* ISBN: *1-59462-250-7* **$27.45**
"Colonel David Crockett was one of the most remarkable men of the times in which he lived. Born in humble life, but gifted with a strong will, an indomitable courage, and unremitting perseverance... Biographies/New Age Pages 424

Lip-Reading *by Edward Nitchie* ISBN: *1-59462-206-X* **$25.95**
Edward B. Nitchie, founder of the New York School for the Hard of Hearing, now the Nitchie School of Lip-Reading, Inc, wrote "LIP-READING Principles and Practice". The development and perfecting of this meritorious work on lip-reading was an undertaking... How-to Pages 400

A Handbook of Suggestive Therapeutics, Applied Hypnotism, Psychic Science ISBN: *1-59462-214-0* **$24.95**
by Henry Munro Health/New Age/Health/Self-help Pages 376

A Doll's House: and Two Other Plays *by Henrik Ibsen* ISBN: *1-59462-112-8* **$19.95**
Henrik Ibsen created this classic when in revolutionary 1848 Rome. Introducing some striking concepts in playwriting for the realist genre, this play has been studied the world over. Fiction/Classics/Plays 308

The Light of Asia *by sir Edwin Arnold* ISBN: *1-59462-204-3* **$13.95**
In this poetic masterpiece, Edwin Arnold describes the life and teachings of Buddha. The man who was to become known as Buddha to the world was born as Prince Gautama of India but he rejected the worldly riches and abandoned the reigns of power when... Religion/History/Biographies Pages 170

The Complete Works of Guy de Maupassant *by Guy de Maupassant* ISBN: *1-59462-157-8* **$16.95**
"For days and days, nights and nights, I had dreamed of that first kiss which was to consecrate our engagement, and I knew not on what spot I should put my lips..." Fiction/Classics Pages 240

The Art of Cross-Examination *by Francis L. Wellman* ISBN: *1-59462-309-0* **$26.95**
Written by a renowned trial lawyer, Wellman imparts his experience and uses case studies to explain how to use psychology to extract desired information through questioning. How-to/Science/Reference Pages 408

Answered or Unanswered? *by Louisa Vaughan* ISBN: *1-59462-248-5* **$10.95**
Miracles of Faith in China Religion Pages 112

The Edinburgh Lectures on Mental Science (1909) *by Thomas* ISBN: *1-59462-008-3* **$11.95**
This book contains the substance of a course of lectures recently given by the writer in the Queen Street Hail, Edinburgh. Its purpose is to indicate the Natural Principles governing the relation between Mental Action and Material Conditions... New Age/Psychology Pages 148

Ayesha *by H. Rider Haggard* ISBN: *1-59462-301-5* **$24.95**
Verily and indeed it is the unexpected that happens! Probably if there was one person upon the earth from whom the Editor of this, and of a certain previous history, did not expect to hear again... Classics Pages 380

Ayala's Angel *by Anthony Trollope* ISBN: *1-59462-352-X* **$29.95**
The two girls were both pretty, but Lucy who was twenty-one who supposed to be simple and comparatively unattractive, whereas Ayala was credited, as her Bombwhat romantic name might show, with poetic charm and a taste for romance. Ayala when her father died was nineteen... Fiction Pages 484

The American Commonwealth *by James Bryce* ISBN: *1-59462-286-8* **$34.45**
An interpretation of American democratic political theory. It examines political mechanics and society from the perspective of Scotsman James Bryce Politics Pages 572

Stories of the Pilgrims *by Margaret P. Pumphrey* ISBN: *1-59462-116-0* **$17.95**
This book explores pilgrims religious oppression in England as well as their escape to Holland and eventual crossing to America on the Mayflower, and their early days in New England... History Pages 268

QTY

The Fasting Cure *by Sinclair Upton*   ISBN: *1-59462-222-1* **$13.95**

In the Cosmopolitan Magazine for May, 1910, and in the Contemporary Review (London) for April, 1910, I published an article dealing with my experiences in fasting. I have written a great many magazine articles, but never one which attracted so much attention... New Age/Self Help/Health Pages 164

Hebrew Astrology *by Sepharial*   ISBN: *1-59462-308-2* **$13.45**

In these days of advanced thinking it is a matter of common observation that we have left many of the old landmarks behind and that we are now pressing forward to greater heights and to a wider horizon than that which represented the mind-content of our progenitors... Astrology Pages 144

Thought Vibration or The Law of Attraction in the Thought World   ISBN: *1-59462-127-6* **$12.95**

by William Walker Atkinson   Psychology/Religion Pages 144

Optimism *by Helen Keller*   ISBN: *1-59462-108-X* **$15.95**

Helen Keller was blind, deaf, and mute since 19 months old, yet famously learned how to overcome these handicaps, communicate with the world, and spread her lectures promoting optimism. An inspiring read for everyone... Biographies/Inspirational Pages 84

Sara Crewe *by Frances Burnett*   ISBN: *1-59462-360-0* **$9.45**

In the first place, Miss Minchin lived in London. Her home was a large, dull, tall one, in a large, dull square, where all the houses were alike, and all the sparrows were alike, and where all the door-knockers made the same heavy sound... Childrens/Classic Pages 88

The Autobiography of Benjamin Franklin *by Benjamin Franklin*   ISBN: *1-59462-135-7* **$24.95**

The Autobiography of Benjamin Franklin has probably been more extensively read than any other American historical work, and no other book of its kind has had such ups and downs of fortune. Franklin lived for many years in England, where he was agent... Biographies/History Pages 332

Name	
Email	
Telephone	
Address	
City, State ZIP	

☐ **Credit Card**   ☐ **Check / Money Order**

Credit Card Number	
Expiration Date	
Signature	

Please Mail to: Book Jungle
PO Box 2226
Champaign, IL 61825
or Fax to: 630-214-0564

ORDERING INFORMATION

web*: www.bookjungle.com*
email*: sales@bookjungle.com*
fax*: 630-214-0564*
mail*: Book Jungle PO Box 2226 Champaign, IL 61825*
or PayPal *to sales@bookjungle.com*

Please contact us for bulk discounts

DIRECT-ORDER TERMS

**20% Discount if You Order
Two or More Books**
Free Domestic Shipping!
Accepted: Master Card, Visa,
Discover, American Express

www.ingramcontent.com/pod-product-compliance
Lightning Source LLC
Chambersburg PA
CBHW081158170626
46813CB00009B/3236